A GRIM FEAST

The town had been torched. Systematically each of the wooden houses had been burnt to the ground. There were few signposts that pointed to the basic definition of the old houses—an arch here, a charred piece of porch there—but mostly the houses were piles of cold, dead, black cinder.

From the corner of his eye Bonner saw movement. The automatic whipped from his pocket and blasted. A vulture exploded in a puff of feathers and blood. The body with a stomach full of rotting flesh thudded to the ground. The sound of the shot raised the clouds of birds that had resettled on the lofty banquet. He raised his gun and was about to blast the birds, fat and lethargic as they were with their picnic. But he stopped himself. The bullets were for men.

A single thought pulsed through the Outrider's brain: Who? Who did this?

BLOOD HIGHWAY [THE]
OUTRIDER

RICHARD HARDING

#3

PINNACLE BOOKS   NEW YORK

THE OUTRIDER #3: BLOOD HIGHWAY

Copyright © 1984 by Robert Tine

An original Pinnacle Books edition, published for the first time anywhere.

First printing/November 1984

ISBN: 0-523-42214-8

Can. ISBN: 0-523-43206-2

Cover art by Michael Meritet

Printed in the United States of America

PINNACLE BOOKS, INC.
1430 Broadway
New York, New York 10018

9 8 7 6 5 4 3 2 1

BLOOD
HIGHWAY

Chapter One

The Hotstates. The Hots, the smugglers and the raiders up in Chicago, the last open city, called them. The Hotstates were a few thousand square miles of the old United States, the lower half of the new continent. There were vast deserts in the west, swamps in the south, and mountains in the east. North of the mountains there was a wide swath of dead ground that marked the border with Leather's slavestates. The Hots were cut in half by a great, wide river that flooded and dried up and overran its banks as it pleased. It had some long screwy Indian name that no one could even remember.

The Hotstates were the personal property of Berger. Not a nice guy, they all said around the bar at Dorca's when his name came up. But nice? Who was nice anymore? If you chose nice as your watchword in life you didn't live long. Or you became some other man's slave. Just as Leather had the Stormers, Berger had the Devils. Not nice guys either, they said at Dorca's.

They talked a lot at Dorca's. Long, meaningless wrangles about who was tougher, Stormers or Devils or Snowmen from the old north west. They talked about the different raiding gangs, who was chickenshit, who was a hard bring down, which ones would stab you in the back for a set of worn old tires. Sometimes, when they knew for sure that he was on the road, they might mention Bonner. Not a nice guy either, someone would whisper. But fair, someone would put in with a look over his shoulder to make sure that Bonner's good buddy Dorca had heard that no one was speaking ill of Bonner, the Outrider.

Over the years Bonner had acquired an almost mythical significance in the minds of the Chicago crew of riders, raiders, crazies, and freaks, the blood-thirsty businessmen who made a living stealing from their better organized neighbors. It looked to them as if Bonner could walk into fire and not smell of smoke when he came out. He tangled with The Leatherman himself and hurt him bad. He had clobbered Devils and Snowmen and the few dumb raiders that thought they had what it took to take Bonner down. But only the dumb and the desperate tried that. You messed with Bonner and you died. It was a simple rule of life, like drinking from a pool of rad-water meant death. Pull a trigger at The Outrider and you had only seconds—if you were unlucky a minute or two—of life left to you. They said that even the rats stayed out of his tumbledown house a few blocks from Dorca's.

"The man can't be brung down," someone would say, "it just ain't a possibility. . . ."

Sometimes Dorca would hear the whispered conversation and he would slam the bar, his bar, with the hefty leg of a pool table that he used to keep order in his joint. Then he would announce why Bonner couldn't be sliced.

"He's smart!" the tank-sized tavernkeeper would bellow. "He's smart! He thinks! He even knows how to read!" Dorca would pause dramatically then pick out a raider, pointing with a finger as thick as a big toe. "And you ain't. You're dumb. You think 'cause you got a gun you can take anybody. Well one day you gonna get your mangy ass sliced into a few pieces. But Bonner is gonna die old and peaceable. . . ."

Everyone agreed that that was probably true. . . .

Bonner was jammed against the overhanging rock a few hundred feet from the waterhole. He had pushed himself into the few inches of shade that the outcrop of giant boulders threw onto the dry brown earth. He didn't want to be seen. The road was somewhere behind him and he could hear the loud voices of the Devils, who, like Bonner, had stopped to get some of the evil-smelling, sticky brown water from the dent in the parched earth. They had found his shark-shaped war wagon packed all over with bloody flanks of beef. The meat was his haul and he was bound for Chicago, battling time and the hot sun, trying to get the precious bloody carcasses home before the heat turned them into a putrid mass of rotting flesh. Bonner had paid for that meat. He had paid for it in the current coin: hours of tracking, blood, bullets, danger. It was his and no Devils were going to rob him of it.

But first he had to concentrate on staying alive. He listened to the shouts of the Devils. They were happy: happy they had come upon some almost fresh food, and happy they had found the car of the raider who had brought it.

"He's gotta be here. Gotta," someone shouted.

"Kill and eat," yelled a happy voice. The Devils made it sound as if they were his two favorite activities. Probably. Though, thought Bonner, rape was probably right up there too.

There was a clatter of heavy boots on loose stones as the Devils fanned out, heading down the slope to the shallow water hole. Bonner pushed himself further against the rock and felt the warmth of the sun-heated stone. He wondered where the Mean Brothers were. The last he had seen of the giant twins they were slopping around in the water. When the Devils had pulled in Bonner had run for the cover of the rocks and lost sight of the Meanies. Bonner wasn't worried about them. If the two mute giants were scared of something Bonner had never seen it. His eyes swept the area in search of them. They were so huge they were pretty hard to hide. Then he saw them and smiled.

The Devils had climbed over the slope that Bonner hid against. They were spread out now in front of the Outrider. Eight. Eight of them wandered towards the water that glittered in front of them.

"He's here somewhere," yelled one, "I can smell him."

There they were a long line of armed men with their backs to him. Bonner silently cursed himself for casually leaving his vicious automatic rifle on the seat of his car. One of these days he was going to get sliced for making a stupid little slip like that, no matter what they said at Dorca's.

He was armed, of course. On one hip he carried his ancient Hi Standard Automatic and his three long, black-handled throwing knives glittered menacingly on the other. Bonner was a master of the silent kill. The thought of Bonner's knives had haunted the frenzied dreams of Stormers, Snowmen, and Devils.

The Hi Standard carried a ten shot clip and it was an excellent rapid fire weapon which in the right hands made sure that the tenth shot was as accurate as the first. If the Devils did nothing more than scatter when the first blood flowed then the huge automatic in Bonner's steady hands would be enough to cut down all eight. It would even leave him the unheard of luxury of two extra shots. But no man just lies there and lets another man kill him—unless he is a fool or a saint. The Devils were neither. The squad leader was carrying an M-16 and if he was any good he would have cut Bonner in half before The Outrider had dropped only six of his fellow Devils. The Devils stared around them. The sun was right over Bonner's shoulder so the outcrop was thrown into a deep vat of shadows.

"Swimmin'!" shouted a Devil and dashed towards the water, casting aside his rifle and the dirty bright orange shirt, the semiofficial uniform of the soldiers of the Hotstates. Caught up in their brother-thug's enthusiasm two other Devils took off after him, breaking the ragged rank in which they walked.

"Doobie!" screamed the squad leader. "We gotta get the man first!"

Ignoring him Doobie shouted: "Last on in is a rotten URK—"

As he splashed into the water what appeared to be two half-submerged boulders baking in the sun grew long hairy arms and caught the three Devils around their filthy necks.

Bonner saw the Mean Brothers go into action and acted himself. Like three steel hornets the knives left Bonner's side. One after another each razor-sharp, blood-lusting blade found and bit Devil flesh. The first neatly pierced the fat roll of flesh on the back of the neck of the squad leader, the knife splitted the throat and carried on splitting the man's prominent Adam's apple. He retched a clot of blood, the wad of gore shooting from his astonished mouth like a bright red liquid bullet. He fell.

The two Devils on either side of him had a second or two to observe their leader dying. Then they took a knife each between the shoulder blades, spine center. Their nervous systems stretched to accommodate the killing injury, then failed, shorting out as they died.

As the first point of the first blade met skin the first hot .22 bullet traveled through the arid morning, screaming unerringly through the air at a Devil. Bonner had figured that the man's brain would register danger before his mind deciphered the impulses. The brain would announce: *Someone is shooting. Get down asshole!* and the big Devil's body would be on its way to the ground before the rest of him knew which way it was headed. But that brain hadn't figured that the sudden steel-jacketed death that threatened out of nowhere was controlled by Bonner. He aimed where he figured the Devil was going, not where he was when the trigger was pulled.

The first .22 slug jammed into the man's mouth making a confused and bloody hash of jawbone, teeth, and tongue before finding a deadly, warm, permanent, cozy home in the soft pink flab of the brain that had been ordering the two hundred forty pound body around a moment before.

The three Devils that had wanted to play in the water were now dying in it. The Mean Brothers, those silent bear-men had risen from the shallows like monsters and caught the playful Devils as if they

7

were children. One Mean had grabbed two and the other had to content himself with one. The three Devils had never been so surprised in their lives and, if the Mean Brothers performed at even half their usual form, they would never be so startled again.

With a grip as strong as steel one of the Mean Brother's hands closed around the throat of the first Devil, the one the squad leader called Doobie. In a single grab his throat closed and cracked; the other arm of the Mean Brother whipped out from his hairy side and clotheslined the second Devil. The man dropped to his knees in the shallow water holding his bruised neck and gagging. The stepping stone-sized foot of the Mean Brother slammed down on his head pushing the Devil's face down into the murky water. All of the cable-strong muscles in the Mean's leg locked holding the Devil's neck under the water. The terror-driven legs of the drowning Devil scissored in the water, the fingers on his hands arced into claws and raked long scratches down the Mean's legs, gouging out long swordlike gouts of flesh from the hairy shin.

The Mean ignored the minor injury and turned his attention to the Devil writhing under the firm grasp that clamped on his neck. He lifted the Devil by the neck and held him up, the man's toes dippling and dabbling just on the surface of the water. The Mean's huge body had become a flesh-and-blood gallows hanging the man from the noose of his left hand. The Devil's face turned red, then blue, then black. Then dead, saliva and spittle spurting from his unnaturally red lips. The Mean let him drop. He raised his foot and the drowned Devil bobbed to the surface like a toy boat.

His brother had gotten rid of his victim with a single huge-fisted blow that had dislodged the Devil's jawbone, driving that sharp shaft of bone up into his brain. The sudden and radical alteration of the man's large features made him look like an old man who had lost his teeth.

Bonner had dropped the other two Devils with unerringly placed slugs. One had torn through a body, twisting up the guts of the deceased like a fork sucking up noodles. It spun round and round until the man's insides were a confused and bloody paste. He gouted blood onto the warm ground, his eyes wide and staring at the white—but quickly darkening—sky. The nerves of his shattered, numb body pulsed in alarm then, like snuffed candles, went out.

The other had taken a clean shot to the head. He died instantly, or almost instantly. He had time to shout: "Mama!" His death came to him like a clock that had been smashed.

The Mean Brothers looked around then, hands on hips, the bodies of their enemies bobbing around them like dead ducks. The brothers looked like hungry kids who couldn't quite believe that all the food was gone. They looked around them hoping that a Devil or two was lurking somewhere. Exactly who the Devils were they didn't know—they were Bonner's enemies and that was good enough for them. If their man wanted them dead then they didn't deserve to live. If more Devils walked the shattered continent then the Mean Brothers figured that it was their duty to find them and kill them. If Bonner wanted them to, of course. He said that they were to live then they lived. The Mean Brothers lived only for Bonner. It was reason enough. They owed him a debt that they could never pay.

Bonner emerged from the shadows. "Sorry, Meanies. That's it. No more. All dead." Bonner walked from body to body retrieving his knives. The Mean Brothers stood in the water, disgusted. They had only bagged three between the two of them. Hardly worth it. They looked enviously at the Boss who had managed six on his own.

"Sorry," yelled Bonner.

The Means shrugged.

Bonner yanked a blade from the lifeless body of the Devil leader. He squatted down and wiped the shaft on the orange shirt. He smiled at the Mean Brothers. In this crazy post-bomb world, he thought, there was no freakier creature than a Mean Brother. Sometimes he wished they could talk so he could know who they were, where they came from. He had found them on the prison island in New York. He had freed them from the Stormers and in return they had dedicated their lives to him. The way he figured it the Means had repaid their debt a thousand times over. Most men would not have bothered to thank him. They stuck by his side. He looked at the dead Devils in the water. He was glad that the Mean Brothers were on his side.

"Hungry?" said Bonner.

The Means nodded. Killing gave them an appetite.

"Well," said Bonner, "let's cut off some steaks and eat."

Chapter Two

One Mean Brother built a fire and the other tore ham-sized steaks off the bloody flank of one of the carcasses draped over the back of Bonner's car.

Bonner himself waded into the water hole and pulled the bodies of the Mean Brothers' victims to shore. To leave them floating in the pool meant poisoning it, and water was too scarce in that part of the world to waste. Suddenly Bonner stopped, still ankle deep in the water. Maybe it would be better. Would it be better, he wondered, to leave the corpses where they fell? Let the hot sun beat down on them, heat the gases within and bloat them until they swelled and burst. Then let the rotting, toxic juices flow from the stinking bodies into the already brackish water. Let them invest the evil liquid with the potential to kill. In his mind's eye Bonner saw, with grim plea-

sure a band of bloodstained, thirsty Devils or Stormers falling upon the water hole and drinking until
their bellies were full.

Then, as the hours passed the creep of death would
slide over them: a sharp cramp—they would think
they had drank too much; then nausea—it would just
be the beginning of a pain-wracked death somewhere
down the road. One less. Maybe two, maybe twenty
fewer evil death dealers—all because Bonner had left
the dead bodies of men like them in the waterhole.
He wouldn't have to waste good bullets. He wouldn't
have to listen to their screams. . . .

But then he thought of the flip side of the question.
What if there was one runaway. A single lone slave
who had made the desperate break for freedom. And
what if he was out of water, wandering in the desert,
death knocking at the door. Then he would see the
waterhole and life would surge through him—with a
taste of that water he would be able to find the
strength to make it to freedom. If Bonner poisoned
the water he would drink it and die. . . .

Bonner decided it would be better to save the one
escapee from tyranny even if it meant letting the
squads of evil men live too. Those men he would
have to kill personally. Let the innocent live. He
would do the dirty work that had to be done to
dispatch the rest.

He pulled the bodies up the slope and left them.
Some sort of desert creature would feast on those
bodies. Let those sharp animal teeth gnaw those

bodies down to the bone. Let the hot sun bleach them white.

A fire was crackling and the blue-red desert night was coming on. Bonner wanted to eat and then get his powerful machine and its precious cargo back onto the road. The roads in the desert were straight and clear. Mounted on the hard nose of his chariot was a powerful spotlight. With it Bonner could cleave the dark of the desert night into two gigantic black blocks. He could make Chicago by morning and get rid of the meat before it turned bad. There were plenty of riders in Chi who would pay a whole raid's worth of money—slates they called them—for a taste of almost fresh beef. The Mean Brothers wouldn't care if he wanted to drive on. They would put up with the bucketing of the car and the roar of the engine. If Bonner knew the Mean Brothers they would fall asleep as if they were in feather beds.

One of the Means had stuck the steaks on the end of pointed sticks and he was grilling the sizzling hunks of meat over the fire. The other brother gestured to Bonner. Come, he was saying, come sit down. Sit with us.

They liked it when Bonner joined them. He would talk to them; about the Outriding days, when men didn't try to kill each other; before the Slavestates, the Hotstates, the Snowstates—before men like Leather and the others. Sometimes, though, during those dark nights he would grow very silent and the Mean Brothers knew he was thinking of Dara. The woman Bonner loved and had been forced to kill.

"Wait," said Bonner to the Meanie's urging that he join them around the fire. Before he lost the light he wanted to go through the saddlebags on the broken down old bikes that the Devils rode. The squad leader's bike was the best of a bad bunch. It was an old Kawasaki missing both fenders. The fuel tank was scratched and dented, the kneepads long gone, and the saddle was torn in places and patched in others. The ignition was just a mass of frayed wires that the rider would touch together to start the thing up. It was plain to Bonner, though, that there wasn't much life left in the machine—the battery was corroded and leaked acid down onto the clutch. Once the electrics went on these bikes they were as good as useless although some skilled mechanics like Lucky could convert them to a kick start. It was an expensive operation.

The decrepitating motorcyle was a good example of a prime rule of life in the post-bomb world. Simpler is better. The delicate electronics and intricate machinery that powered the old world were as good as useless in the new world. Keep things simple and you survived—maybe. The Devil squad leader would have found himself with a couple of hundred pounds of unstartable bike on his hands when his wiring finally went. A rider with a brutish old kick start Harley or Triumph could go on riding until someone killed him.

The saddlebags yielded little: a faded Hertz Number One Club (number one what, Bonner wondered) road map with the impassible roads and the rad-water lakes marked in grimy grease pencil. A pair of riding gloves split at the fingers. A nicked and scarred handgun, it looked like a .38, the barrel wound round with a double length of rusty wire. Bonner wouldn't have pulled the trigger if his life had depended on it. Plainly he had run into one of Berger's skag battalions. They were the bully boys that Berger used to keep the slaves in line and for other all brawn-no-brains duties—escort, torture, guarding something or somebody. The other half of Berger's army was a little better. He divided his men into two sections: skag and silk. The silks were better trained and better equipped. The skags hated the silks and tried to outdo their betters in ferocity. The silks hated the skags and did their best to ignore them. Neither type of crew was the sort you would want to meet in a dark alley.

The saddlebags of the other bikes yielded little as well. A gray hunk of bread, some ammunition, a heavy coat, a bed roll alive with lice . . . typical skag.

It was in the last bag that he found something that made his blood run cold. It made him glad, suddenly, that out there in the darkness lay the bodies of the eight Devils. It was a gun. A tiny little pea shooter of a rifle. A kid's gun . . . Carved into the stock, a cheap sliver of wood as thin as a teenage girl's shoulder blade were three words. The carving was crude but the pride in the words was writ large: BOBBY. HIS GUN.

Bonner stared at the writing. He knew the gun. He knew the hand, the young hand that had carved his name there.

No, thought Bonner. It can't be.

The Mean Brothers sensed Bonner's sudden change of mood. They watched him for a moment. He was staring at the gun. They got up from the fire and padded to his side and gently took the gun from him. They looked at it, then at each other and shrugged. The little rifle and the carving on it meant nothing to them. But it plainly meant something to Bonner. He straightened up, tall against the night sky. He retrieved the gun from the Mean Brother.

"Look," he said gesturing towards the cooling meat, "you better eat that while we're moving."

The Means nodded. An interrupted dinner was a small price to pay for Bonner's companionship and friendship.

Chapter Three

Bonner slid behind the wheel of his road master and simultaneously hit the starter and the spotlight. A great valley of white light appeared in front of the car, like a shining road to paradise; but Bonner wasn't fooled. He knew that there was no paradise in this dirty world. That shimmering bright highway was merely the path to a thousand miles of death and blood. It was the road the Outrider always traveled. A thoroughfare of vengeance.

He pushed his vehicle out onto the cracked roadway and hit top speed in seconds. The throaty roar opened up from the twin upswept exhaust pipes, echoing through the blue-black night. The huge Mean Brothers were packed into the back of the bullet car, resting against a bloody side of beef, munching happily on their steaks. Above their heads like a black halo arched the rollbar of the machine. Anchored to it, nose down, was Bonner's major piece of artillery, a worn old .50-caliber machine gun. He used it rarely, but when he did his enemies fell in hordes.

The car was simple: engine, gun, fuel tank, and room enough for some cargo. It had been built for Bonner by Lucky, the best mechanic on the continent. It got Bonner where he wanted to go and it got him there fast. It could outrun anything on those dangerous roads—but Bonner didn't use it for running much.

He was on the road now, eating up the miles. The Outrider stared into the bright valley carved by his spotlight. As always, he wondered what the broken white line down the middle of the road meant. . ...
Then he drifted into thoughts of his own.

BOBBY. HIS GUN.

There was a place . . . Bonner gripped the wheel tighter in rage. It was the only sign he gave of the fury that was building within him.

There was a place . . . A place a couple of days' ride away, a place to the east of the point Bonner was at then, a place far from the desert. A few riders knew about it and they kept it secret. They called it by a special, funny name. . . .

BOBBY. HIS GUN.

The place was called Almost Normal. Someone had put a sign on the road on the outskirts of the village: ALMOST NORMAL. USA. USA. Bonner liked that.

Bobby was a kid, a boy of fourteen, maybe fifteen. His father was called Charlie. He was a big, strong, happy man. He was the richest man Bonner knew. Richer than Leatherman and Berger with all their gold and gas and girls and slaves. Richer than Bonner who could measure his wealth in power and the fear other men held him in. Charlie had Bobby and Bobby's mother, a gentle woman called Martha, and a daughter Emily. They were a family, one of eighty or ninety who lived in Almost Normal. They had a life they enjoyed living. It was a life that, as the name of the town put it, was almost normal.

Almost Normal was up in some smoky mountains in the space between the Hotstates and the Slavestates. If those two powers knew the tiny hamlet was there they didn't seem to care. Almost Normal was too small, too far away to bother with. It was hard to get to, it was poor. Who cares?

No, it wasn't rich and it wasn't big but it had something that the rest of the continent, maybe the rest of the world, didn't have. It was free. It was peaceful. The men didn't carry guns, except to hunt. They weren't violent, they didn't have to be.

And there were kids. Children. New life. Boys and girls who knew no other world than the placid life of Almost Normal. The boys hunted with their fathers and grew strong. The girls learned skills from their mothers and were pretty and gentle and, in their own way, as strong as their menfolk. Bonner had read once about a race of people called Americans who held as their heroes some hardy types called pioneers.

When Bonner thought of pioneers he thought of the people of Almost Normal.

Almost Normal might have been the past as Bonner read about it but he hoped, he wished, that it could be the future too. There was a seductive quality about the little town that he found almost irresistible. When he was at his lowest he would go there and drink in the sustaining atmosphere of peace and harmony. Sometimes he could hardly pull himself away to rejoin the harsh, brutal world that he lived in.

"Stay with us," Charlie had said the last time Bonner passed through. "Give up the violent life. We'll find you a wife. Live here with us. You'll have a home. . . ."

A home. The words flashed through Bonner's mind with the ferocity of one of his killing blades. The idea of having a home was almost unimaginable. He had four broken rooms in the ruins in Chicago. Four old rooms that caught the sound of the late night brawls at Dorcas; screams as the streetworkers took someone down with a rusty knife or a bullet. Home, where there was always someone's fresh corpse outside the door. That was home.

Martha had joined her husband to plead with him. "Stay here with us. We could help you. You could help us. The kids love you . . . Stay."

Reflected in the blinding light Bonner could see Martha's face, strong and gentle.

But something had drawn Bonner back to the road, to the violent life he hated. It had become a drug, this need to ride, to kill, to blindly avenge. It was his work, his mission, his calling. To settle down in Almost Normal would have been a betrayal, a violation of his impassioned oath, the one he had made on the graves and memories of his dead friends and the thousand of innocents he did not know who had died or who were enslaved. He could not stop. He had promised Dara.

Bobby was just a kid. Bonner had taught him how to shoot. And he had taught him how to write. Bonner asked him once which skill he valued most. "I need them both," the kid had said. BOBBY. HIS GUN.

Now his gun with his writing on it had turned up in the saddlebag of a skag-Devil's clapped out MC. Bonner hoped fervently that some intricate system of barter had carried the .22 far away from Bobby and Almost Normal. Maybe Bobby had traded it with a rider for a better gun and in turn maybe that rider passed it on to someone else and so on until it ended up with the dead Devil. Maybe . . .

But Bonner doubted it. Somehow he knew that a terrible force had swept down on that peaceful community and torn it apart. The real world, the real future had caught up with Almost Normal. Bonner knew that the world would not see its like again.

Those who ruined that tiny island of peace and calm were dead men. The Outrider decreed it.

Chapter Four

Wiggy heard the engine, muffled at first in the dawn air, but getting louder a lot faster than he liked.

He said: "Fuck." And then he almost dropped the bucket of gasoline he had just hoisted up from the oasis. It was a Devil fuel dump he was stealing from and if that engine he could so plainly hear belonged to a Devil or a friend of theirs then there was going to be trouble and trouble was the last thing Wiggy wanted. He had plenty of that already.

His hands were trembling so bad he slopped gasoline all over the tank of the little brute of a car he was trying to nourish. The gas went everywhere but down the narrow mouth of the gas tank.

"Damn, damn, damn," said Wiggy, his voice quavering in fear.

The vehicle was as weird as Wiggy was. It was a

three-wheeler of almost laughable design. A triangular chassis with two fat tires up front and a single wheel behind supported a seat and the two engines. At the rear, behind the driver's seat was a gas-powered generator. In the snubbed prow of the car sat an electric motor that must have been stolen from the housing of an elevator or some other heavy piece of electrical machinery. The generator generated the power which drove the electric motor which powered the car. The whole thing was connected to a primitive drive train by belts that would burn your hand off if you touched one while the whole thing was running. The rider who sold it to him told Wiggy that the rig needed practically no gas to keep it moving. He lied.

Not only did Wiggy's wagon need as much gas as everybody else's machine, the three-wheeler was noisy, slow, unreliable, heavy, and hard to drive. Most of the time Wiggy hated the thing. But sometimes he loved it. It was his and it meant he wasn't a raider anymore. But was that such a good thing? Right then all he wanted was his old bike and his old gang.

Wiggy had been a raider in an outfit called Pershing's Pistoleroes (whatever the hell a pistolero was) but he had had ambition. He didn't want to be a raider. He wanted to be a smuggler and make himself some real profit. There were twenty pistoleroes and Wiggy didn't like splitting the share twenty ways. It only dawned on him after he was on his own that he hadn't done a whole hell of a lot to earn his share but it was too late for that now. So he set himself up to ride alone. He needed money so he sold his reliable old cycle—an iron creature made up of a half a dozen major spare parts from other bikes—and used the money to buy himself about a ton and a half of ammunition and his strange little vehicle. With a dismissive sneer—"So long, assholes"—Wiggy left the Pistoleroes and struck out on his own.

This was his first ride and he wasn't having much luck. He got lost a lot. His dreams of returning to Chi with gas or something equally valuable had long since faded. He just couldn't find anything. He couldn't even find trouble. Wiggy figured he was the only rider on the continent who hadn't been shot at recently. The world was one big empty space filled with dead ground and dead ruins.

He still had the ammunition he had equipped himself with and he figured he was going to head back to Chicago and say that he found it someplace and sell it as if it had been his haul. Then he would put it around that he wouldn't mind joining the Pistoleroes again, just for a couple of rides. The truth of it was the emptiness, the loneliness of a single-handed ride scared him. It was worse than running into a bunch of Stormers or Devils—almost.

A big trouble with his crazy little car was that it was hard to start. It was the rule of simplicity taken to a ridiculous extreme. To turn the generator over you had to swing a crank and the engine was always, but always, reluctant to catch. This little feature made a quick getaway a little hard to pull off.

The fuel flopped everywhere. The engine was getting louder.

"Fuck it!" screamed Wiggy, throwing the bucket aside, splashing gas everywhere. He dove for the crank and swung it and in the process scraped most of the skin off the back of his left hand. He yelped in pain and tried again. This time the generator rewarded him with a few taunting tut-tut noises and died.

"Fuck you," he bellowed. He kicked the machine as hard as he could. The approaching engine seemed to fill his ears.

"Okay," he said, "I'll fight it out." He pulled a long barrel rifle from behind the seat and scampered away behind some of the rubble that had once been the gas station. He found some cover behind the metal sign that had fallen into the station forecourt. It read MOBIL.

Wiggy put a round in the chamber and told himself that anybody who came round that corner was going to buy a slug. "Dead meat," he said between clenched teeth.

"I don't care if it's my fuckin' mother. Blow her head off," he said to make himself feel better.

Then he noticed something. The silence. The sound of the engine had vanished. Gone. One minute it had seemed as if the car had been right on top of him, just around the corner, now nothing. Had he really heard it?

"Gotta stop drinking that shit," he said referring

to the only companion he had had on his lonely trip. It was a jug of raw alcohol that he had bought from Dorca and that he soused himself with every night.

"Stuff makes you crazy," he whispered as if it was secret information. Although, right then he would have given anything for a drink. The thought inspired such sudden and violent longing in his mind that he thought about risking a dash to his car to get the earthenware flagon that he could see tantalizingly close. It was peeping out from the huge bale of ammunition.

"There was nobody coming," he said as if to explain unseen judges why he was giving up his position for a swig of that tongue barbeque he carried around with him. He strolled out from behind the Mobil sign, grabbed the flagon, and stuck the cork in his ear. He did that so later, when he was drunk, he would know where he had put it. He lifted the jug and took a deep pull. He held it in his mouth a second and then shivered as he swallowed the fire-hot liquid. His eyes rolled in his head and he stamped his feet a couple of times in a happy little frolicsome dance of pain.

"Ahhhhhhh," he said happily. He looked analytically at the jug and wondered what the hell Dorca made this shit out of. For a second he thought about the chances of running his little machine on it if he ever got low on gas.

The jug made a second trip to his lips. "Hell," he said, "it might be better, as a rule, to drink the gas

and use Dorca's swill on the piece of shit engine.''
He laughed out loud at his little joke. Life suddenly
looked better.

On the third trip to his mouth catastrophe struck. In
fact, a bullet hit his jug. The liquor poured onto him
drenching him from head to foot. He damn near shit
his pants. The raw alcohol got into his eyes and set
them on fire, or at least that's what it felt like. He
rolled around on the ground howling in pain, rubbing
his burning eyes to clear them of the pain. When he
regained his sight he managed to focus on a man
standing over him. The man had a fistful of automatic.

Holy shit, thought Wiggy. It's Bonner. "Hi," he
said lamely.

"Where's Pershing?" asked The Outrider.

"I ain't with him no more," stammered Wiggy.

"I don't know your name," said Bonner.

Jeez, thought Wiggy as the Mean Brothers wandered up. He's got his doom freaks with him. Wiggy
had seen the Mean Brothers in Dorca's drinking beaker after beaker of Dorca's best booze—on the house
because they were with Bonner, the lucky fucks—but
they never got drunk. They would put away twenty
or thirty each and stare at their glasses and at each
other unable to see what all the fuss was about. As if
drinking was a game they couldn't get the hang of
with rules they didn't understand.

"I asked your name," said Bonner.

"Wiggy."

"Pleased to meet you, Wiggy."

"Likewise," said Wiggy. "Look, can I stand up?"

"Sure."

Wiggy rose slowly as if afraid that a sudden movement would set off the Hi Standard without any good reason.

"That your rig?" asked Bonner.

"Yessir." He paused a moment. "Where's yours? I heard it coming . . ."

"I stopped a ways down the road. No sense in driving into a surprise."

"Nope. Nope. Guess not." Wiggy took off his shirt. It had been drenched with liquor and the fumes were beginning to make him feel woozy. Wiggy was nervous. Bonner seemed friendly enough but you could never tell with a bullet eater like him. Hoping Bonner wouldn't notice, Wiggy placed the frayed cuff of his denim shirt to his mouth and sucked out some of the liquor. The taste on his tongue revived him.

"See you got yourself some ammunition."

"That's right."

"Got something for this?" Bonner held up his automatic.

"Yes, I believe I do."

"Something for a shotgun?"

"That too. If the gauge ain't that big."

"No problem."

"Look, you want it," said Wiggy, "you take it. On me." A couple more inches of sleeve went into his mouth.

"Could you take your shirt out of your mouth?"

"I said, it's yours. Take it."

"I'm not going to steal it," said Bonner.

"Oh yeah, oh yeah, I know that," said Wiggy quickly, affably. "You ain't gonna steal it. It's a uh, a watchamacallit, y'know, a loan. When we meet in Chicago, hey pay me back. You know, when you can. No problem. No hurry." Please thought Wiggy, just take the fuckin ammo and get out of here.

"No," said Bonner.

"No," agreed Wiggy quickly, "I guess not." He shrugged his shoulders. "Hey, you win some, you lose some." He reached for his shirt. Suddenly he felt pretty silly. He was standing there his thin white chest sticking out and with a cork in his ear giving away all his worldly possessions to the meanest man on the continent. He took the cork out of his ear but it didn't make him feel any better.

"I'll trade you," said Bonner. "I have a couple of sides of beef on my rig. I don't need them where I'm going. I need your ammo. You're bound for Chi, right?"

"Right!"

"Then you can haul this beef with you. If you hurry, it won't spoil."

"Meat?"

"Yep."

"You want to trade me meat for ammo."

"S'right."

"Where'd you get it."

32

"Texas."

"Deal." Wiggy was already framing the story. 'Yeah, I headed down to Texas. Got some meat. Headed back. Simple . . .'

Wiggy helped Bonner and the Mean Brothers move the heavy slabs of grey meat. "So where you headed?" he asked as he and Bonner were equals.

"No place you ever heard of," said Bonner knowing they weren't.

When the exchange of cargoes had been completed and Bonner had topped up his tank Wiggy stood around waiting for the Outrider to get in his big powerful rig and get the hell out of there. He didn't want to be humiliated by that damn ornery crank in front of Bonner.

"See ya," yelled Wiggy over the boom of Bonner's engine.

Bonner waved.

"Hey," shouted Wiggy, "I just got one question. Why did you blow away my jug."

"I wanted to see your face," yelled Bonner. Then he slammed his car into gear and took off. The little rider had provided him with enough firepower to protect himself. He pointed the sharp nose of his car down the road. Almost Normal was his next stop.

Wiggy watched him go. "He wanted to see my face," he said, "what an asshole . . ."

He got his funny little rig going faster and easier than he thought, almost as if the car had been scared by Bonner and wanted to get the hell out of there as fast as it could. But the spirit of cooperation didn't last. Wiggy had travelled about twenty miles when the oil feed that lubricated the armature on the motor parted forever. In another mile the engine seized and billowed black smoke all over the place. The car coasted to a halt and died.

By nightfall Wiggy was weeping, a wreck. He had taken the engine apart and put it back together twice and nothing. The whole idiotic contraption had given up the ghost at last. And the meat was beginning to smell suspicious. Goddam, he could use a drink.

==Chapter Five

Almost Normal was gone and in its place stood a dark, silent skeleton—the last remains of a village that had died a sudden and painful death. The savagery that had visited Almost Normal seemed to have done more than swept away the hamlet and its inhabitants, it seemed to have altered the ground on which it stood. Had Bonner not known where Almost Normal had lain he would have driven right past it. Now it looked like nothing more than one of a million other rubble villages that were scattered all over the continent.

Even when Almost Normal had been a place of the living it hadn't been much to look at. The whole town was a couple of streets each a few hundred yards long. Fronted on each street were a few rows of neat, simple houses each sitting in the middle of its own tidy garden. In the center of the village had been a tall, wide-branched tree. Somehow that tree, pre-bomb by centuries, came to be the heart of the town. It was there that the whole town would meet. They came there on warm summer evenings, a simple communal social event to talk or to hear one of the older men tell stories of times that none of them could remember. It was beneath those all embracing limbs that the town was governed: where they decided how the food and the work was to be divided. Somehow that tree made them all feel safe, protected, at home.

Bonner could remember nights when he had sat there with them, the whole village hushed as he told them of the world beyond their borders. They could never quite believe his tales of war and tyranny and disaster. Men were not as bad as Bonner painted them, they thought. They learned that he had spoken the unvarnished truth.

It was not until he saw the tree that Bonner finally admitted to himself that he was in fact in Almost Normal.

As he approached the tree, the branches seemed to come alive. It was as if a sudden and strong wind had come up out of nowhere and was now whistling through those thick branches. All at once it seemed that the wind was blowing huge black leaves into the sky. But the day was still.

Then he saw. Vultures, disturbed by the roar of his engine were temporarily forsaking the vast and bloody feast hanging in the branches. Suspended in the tree limbs were the stiff and mutilated bodies of a dozen people. As the vultures took to the sky wheeling, watching until it was safe to land and eat again, a score of rat's heads appeared from tattered fleshy holes in the corpses looking out to see what all the fuss was about.

It was impossible to say who the bodies had been or even which were men and which were women. The birds and the rats had ripped and torn until the corpses were bloody tattered scarecrows. The soft parts had gone first: eyes, cheeks, genitals . . . Then they went for the bellies and the chests. Bonner turned away.

The Mean Brothers looked very grave. Unable to speak they had somehow developed a sense that could filter emotion almost from the air. Almost Normal was as still as death, but in the aura of the dead village the mute giants could feel the terrible disturbance of sudden, screaming death. The evil that had been done there would mark and stain the earth. The tree would die of it—and even if the world reestablished itself as a place of peace and harmony that spot where Almost Normal stood would always be barren of life and feeling.

The town had been torched. Systematically each of the frail wooden houses had been burnt to the ground. There were few signposts that pointed to the basic definition of the old houses—an arch here, a charred piece of porch there—but mostly the houses were piles of cold, dead, black cinder.

Stretched as an anguished last clutch at life a charred hand had thrust itself from the burnt rubble. The baking heat of the burning building had gnarled and twisted the bone of the arm. Something had been gnawing at the blackened fingertips. The bones showed gray against the black ash. Whose hand had that been? A mother's, a soft hand that smoothed a child's brow? A husband's who had clasped his wife's hand on a summer night under the tree . . .

Bonner stopped the car and got out. Cinders crackled under his feet and he walked slowly to the charred ruins of the house that had been Martha and Charlie's home. There was no sign that the people who lived there might still be alive.

From the corner of his eye he saw movement. The automatic whipped from his pocket and blasted. A vulture exploded in a puff of feathers and blood. The body with a stomach full of rotting human flesh thudded to the ground. The sound of the shot raised the cloud of birds that had resettled on their lofty banquet. Bonner raised his gun and was about to blast the birds, fat and lethargic as they were with their picnic. But he stopped himself. The bullets were for men.

A sleek gray family of rats bustled by as if they were late for an appointment.

Bonner was no stranger to death, but the complete, savage destruction of Almost Normal shook him to the core of his soul. He felt his body filling with liquid hate. It was hotter, stronger, and more bitter than the foulest of the brews served up at Dorca's.

A single word, a single thought pulsed through the Outrider's brain:

Who?

Who did this? Who fell upon this peaceful place and destroyed it? Bonner did not care if there was a "why." There was no why. There could be no reason by which anyone could justify doing this. Evil like this could not be explained. When—and the day would come and soon too—when Bonner had found the evildoers, when he had them in the sights of his weapon he would hear no reasons, no excuses. He would pull the trigger, he would destroy them without a second thought. They had had their fun. Their actions were history now—no words could erase their sins. Now they had to pay the price. Bonner had already added up the bill, a simple calculation: They must pay with their lives.

But first he had to find them. He noticed that the ground was deeply furrowed with the tire marks of dozens of vehicles, cycles, and cars. But that told him little. It could have been Stormers or Devils or Raiders. There were dozens of murdering bands roaming the ruined roads and any one of them could have done this. Raiders might have burned the town, but Bonner, knowing how the Raiders worked, doubted it. A burned town would produce no more so they could not come back and steal again. Raiders killed but they wouldn't kill everybody. Someone had to be left behind to build up the town again. Besides, Almost Normal was too far off the beaten track for Raiders.

Stormers killed everything that moved. And for no good reason. So did Devils.

Then it struck Bonner. There were very few bodies. There were the bodies in the tree and the single charred corpse. Almost Normal had a couple of hundred people. . . .

"Meanie, do me a favor and get your shovel," asked Bonner of the Mean Brother. When they bothered to use weapons the Mean Brothers used a shovel and an axe respectively.

The Mean returned with the shovel and Bonner took it from him and began to dig in the charred ruins of the house nearest him. He used the spade to turn over the rubble, searching the burnt wood methodically searching for the remains of the villagers. He moved from house to house and indeed found some bodies. A man here, a woman there. He stopped dead for a few minutes to recover from the shock of finding a baby's burnt body.

After an hour of digging Bonner leaned on the shovel. He wiped his brow and wondered if he should feel happy or sad for the residents of Almost Normal. Not many of them had died, their bodies were nowhere to be found. That only meant one thing. Slavers. They had been carried off by one of the slave raiding parties. It had been a large one, it would have to have been to carry off the men, women, and children of Almost Normal. That meant Stormers or Devils. Bonner knew how they treated their captives. If they took fifty and twenty made it to market they considered that they had done a pretty fine job of driving. Percentages of dead were sometimes much higher. Sometimes they would take fifty and fifty would die. . . .

Bonner looked around him and wondered if he should feel happy for the survivors. Now he had to find them and fast, before they all died on the road.

"Come on, Means," he said. "Time to go."

The Mean Brothers took their places in the car, glad to be leaving this place.

Bonner started up the engine and the vultures swirled into the sky again. He drove down the hill slowly, his heart heavy. Almost Normal was really almost normal now—because normality was measured not in peace and happiness but in war, death, and pain. Finally the little community was in step with the rest of the dying world.

Chapter Six

Bonner was silent as he negotiated his big vehicle down the steep twisted road that led down the hill from Almost Normal. Every second took him further from that black place but the spirit of hell and horror he had found there seemed to follow him, to suffocate him like a poison smoke. It would be a very long time before the hateful image of that dead place ceased to torment him. Revenge would go a long way towards soothing him but even then it would not be enough. The Mean Brothers could sense Bonner's seething anger, his torturing pain.

They were relieved when Bonner spoke. "You see the tracks?" He slowed down slightly and pointed at the dirt road rushing under them. "See them?"

The Mean Brothers nodded.

"Stormers or Devils . . . We won't know until we

see if they cut north or south. North means we are following Stormers. South, Devils."

The Mean Brothers nodded again.

"We're going to follow them. Devils, Stormers, it doesn't matter . . ."

The Mean Brothers shook their huge heads again. Nope. As far as they were concerned it didn't matter. An enemy was an enemy. They only ceased being an enemy when the Mean Brothers had dealt with them in their own way.

"And when we find them, we are going to kill them," said Bonner. A few seconds of silence followed and then he added: "All of them . . ."

The Means nodded and grinned again. They were always up for a fight.

They wound down the mountain, the Mean Brothers following the tracks very closely. Bonner studied them too, trying to learn from them. He wished Beck was there. Beck was a giant smuggler who could follow a man over water if he put his mind to it. Bonner was good, but Beck was better.

Bonner stared at the snaky gray marks in the gray dust of the rocky road. Where other men would have only seen a tangle of confused tire tracks Bonner saw a whole story. There were at least six trucks, their heavy treads easily recognizable to the trained eye, and there were at least two dozen motorcycles. A big force, certainly one large enough to take a peaceful town.

Bonner stared down at the tracks. He drove with

both hands on the wheel but he kept his head crooked over the minimal bodywork of his car watching the road surface. At the end of those tracks, somewhere up ahead, maybe ten miles, maybe a hundred, his enemy was waiting for the destiny that The Outrider was meant to bring him.

A Mean Brother tapped Bonner on the shoulder. Bonner looked up. A few yards ahead of him, looming large in the failing light, lay a pile of logs. It blocked the road completely. Bonner could feel the Mean Brothers tense as if the matted hair on their huge bodies raised itself like the fur on a dog.

Ambush. Bonner reacted, channeling his unfailing animal sense of action perfectly. The car slammed into reverse sped back a few yards then, from out of the gloom behind him a fat log swung out of the trees that overhung the road.

The heavy shaft of wood clanged into Bonner's fuel tank and was stopped dead by the tough pipe rollbar. The log swung back as if it was a giant pendulum, then the vines that suspended it broke and fell athwart the road behind him. To reverse over it Bonner had to push his car a few feet forward to give himself some running room. As he hit reverse again a shotgun blast rocketed out of the gloom and tore up the light canvas fender that protected the right front tire.

The gunman had made a mistake. He had fired both barrels at once and he had missed. Bonner heard it and so did the Mean Brothers. It was a simple error but one that inevitably spelt death on the road. The Means were over the side of the car, dashing for the light of the muzzle flash that still seemed to hang in the air. Unless the shooter had a back-up piece of artillery or could reload as fast as Bonner himself, the Mean Brothers had him.

"Alive!" ordered Bonner. He picked up his lethal, sharp-snouted automatic machine gun, the Steyr AUG. It could pepper lead into the area as fast as it took to sneeze.

In the darkness Bonner could hear the crack of a gun barrel as it was smashed hard on the rocks by the side of the road. That was a Mean Brother neutralizing a threat. This sound was followed by a heavy smack, an open handed blow to a jaw. Then there came a tiny, girlish sob.

Bonner hit the light on his wagon. The white beam shot out and caught two very puzzled-looking Mean Brothers. Each held a child by the scruff of the neck. A boy and a girl. Bonner's heart gave a little leap. Dangling a full foot above the dirt road were Bobby and Emily, Charlie and Martha's kids. Emily was choking back tears and her white jaw glowed red where the Mean had belted her. Bobby stared defiantly into the white light.

Before Bonner could speak, Bobby's hand dived into the pocket of his worn homespuns and pulled out a knife. Wriggling in the Mean Brother's firm grasp, he tried to jam into his captor's chest. The Mean Brother's unoccupied hand swept up, grabbed Bobby's wrist as if his huge hand was a handcuff. The Mean Brother squeezed, but not nearly as hard as he could have. The kid cried out and let the knife fall.

The Mean caught it before it hit the ground, stuck the blade into his mouth, clenched his teeth over the steel like a pirate, and then bent it into a neat U with his free hand. He flung the knife into the darkness and shook Bobby like a pissed-off mother: Behave, he was saying. Stop trying to kill me.

"Put 'em down, Means," commanded Bonner. The Mean Brothers carefully put their captives on the ground. They could tell by Bonner's tone of voice that he was inclined to be friendly to the kids.

Bobby and Emily drew together, tense. Bobby looked into the light then around at the Mean Brothers, as if pondering the chance of running for it.

Bonner stepped out of the light, walking towards them.

"Bobby?" he said softly, "Emily? Do you remember me?"

Bobby's blue eyes grew wide. "Mr. Bonner?" he said as if he could hardly believe it.

"That's right," said Bonner. No sooner had the words left his lips than Bonner found his strong arms full of two sobbing kids.

The Mean Brothers smiled, pleased at their boss' sudden embarrassment. One Mean leaned against the other and they both smiled as if to say: That's so nice . . .

Emily had squirmed into his arms and clung tight

to his neck. He could feel her hot little tears wetting the side of his face. Bobby grasped the Outrider's callused hand as if he could never let go.

Bonner had no experience of children and he groped for the words, something to say that might reassure them that they were safe with him. He could think of nothing save to murmur over and over again: "Okay, it's okay . . ." But they hardly heard him. Just being there was enough for them. They wanted nothing more than a friendly face and an adult to give some sort of order to their lives. Bonner was the best they could have hoped for. A friend. A friend with a gun and a knowledge of the world to protect them.

Slowly Bonner uncoiled their desperate embraces and as he did so he motioned to the Means to build a fire. The kids were shivering in shock and fear—two people never looked so helpless, and for a second Bonner marveled that they had been able to survive for as long as they had.

Then Bonner remembered the artfully set ambush and the sudden and almost deadly accurate fire from the early evening gloom. The Outrider smiled to himself. What would Dorca or Beck or poor old dead Starling say if they knew that the great Bonner had almost got sliced by a fifteen-year-old kid who probably had a bruise the size of a pie pan on his shoulder where the old smooth bore had kicked back.

The Mean Brothers kicked together a fire in no time and the five of them gathered around it. Bonner had saved a few pieces of meat from the haul and he had a can of pre-bomb string beans someplace and the Mean Brothers set about preparing a meal. They worked with as much care as their massive hands could bring to the task. The steaks were as tough as old shoes now but the smell of them roasting over the fire caught in the kids' noses and they eyed the spitting hunks hungrily.

As the Mean Brothers worked they shot quick, curious glances at Bobby and Emily. Kids were rare in the new world and the Mean Brothers looked at them as if unable to make up their minds if the two teenagers were in fact children or some sort of adult arrested at some strange point in their development.

Bobby and Emily looked unabashedly at the Mean Brothers. If kids were rare, specimens like the Mean Brothers were rarer.

Bobby was blond and square-faced, tall for his age, which Bonner estimated to be somewhere around fifteen. He had the look of a kid who had known hard work from an early age. Martha and Charlie had taught their children well. They were polite, dutiful, and loving, qualities you didn't see much of these days, Bonner reflected.

Emily had dark hair and blue eyes and there was a firm cast to her chin that spoke of a tendency to defiance. Bonner could see in her fragile features the promise of radiant beauty in her future. If she had a future. If anyone had . . .

Gradually, slowly, as if not to alarm them, Bonner drew the details of the raid on Almost Normal out of them. They spoke hesitantly and if they were afraid fo stirring up a distant but dreadful nightmare.

Bobby did most of the talking with Emily adding pieces of information as she recalled them.

"It was almost night," said Bobby, rubbing some of the beef grease from his chin. "The men were on their way back from the fields. . . ."

"When," asked Bonner, "when was this?"

Emily and Bobby looked at him blankly.

"How long ago? How many nights have you been out here? How long have you been alone?"

"Five nights," said Emily firmly.

Five nights in the wild, thought Bonner. These kids were a lot stronger than they looked. Of course, they came from hardy, self-reliant stock. Five nights . . . That was bad news for Bonner, though. That meant that the marauders had a hell of a lead on them. If they were Stormers they were probably deep in the Slavestates now. Probably, they were approaching The Cap, the ruined white marble city-*cum*-tomb from which Leatherman ruled his domain.

"We heard their engines," said Bobby. "Everyone stopped where they were and listened. I think . . . I think some of the men, like Dad, they knew there was trouble coming. . . ."

"Some of them went and got their guns," put in Emily.

Their guns, thought Bonner. A few old hunting weapons nothing that would hold up a determined band of raiders for more than a few seconds. Even if every man in Almost Normal had been armed some Stormers of silk-Devils would have cut them up in no time flat.

"Where were you?" asked Bonner.

"I was digging the yard," said Bobby. "Emily was with Mama in the kitchen."

"They came straight into town. The noise . . ." Emily searched for the words. ". . . the noise, it filled everything. It was everywhere. . . ."

"One of them, a leader, I guess, went up to Ralph Woods. I saw him. He just went up to him and just shot him. While he was standing there. Just shot him, for no reason . . ." Bobby's voice strained and cracked but he kept his tears in check. Bonner figured that the death of Ralph Woods was the first time that young Bobby had ever witnessed an act of wanton cruelty. It would not be the last.

"Some shouted 'Round them up' " said Emily, looking over to her brother as if expecting him to confirm her words.

"How many," Bonner asked. "How many men were there?"

"I dunno," said Bobby, "a lot."

"Emily?"

"Yes. A lot. I don't know exactly how many."

"Were they dressed in any special way? You know, a uniform or something like that?"

"Orange shirts," said Bobby firmly.

"Devils," said Bonner to the Mean Brothers. They

shrugged. The brand of their victims was of little interest to them. Just so long as they found them and killed them the Mean Brothers were happy.

The whole story spun out slowly. The kids would start then stop when the details of the story became too much for them to bear.

In the confusion they had become separated from their mother and father. Bobby had hid in the crawlspace under their modest house. Emily had hid under the stairs. The Devils had searched every house before torching them but they were in a hurry and it was the people of Almost Normal they wanted, not their meagre possessions. Both children had fled from the commotion away from the gangs of men in the main street. They had hidden in the woods—the Devils hadn't bothered with a perimeter guard—and they spent the night listening to the screams and watching as the black night sky turned orange as the flames consumed their village. Gradually the screams died away and the sky turned pink with the glow of the dawn.

"When it was light, we went back."

Bonner thought of the horror of the dozens of people hanging from the tree. "You went back? Why?"

"To find Momma and Poppa," said Emily matter of factly.

"And did you?"

"No. They were gone." Bobby's voice was flat and dull and sounded in those moments like that of a very old man.

Bonner was relieved. None of the bodies in the tree were those of his friends. He realized now who those poor dead people were. They were the few old men and women of Almost Normal, some of the few people on the continent to make it to old age. They were honored and taken care of by the younger inhabitants of the hamlet, paid homage for their age and wisdom. But to Devil slavers they were just human garbage. The men were too weak to work. The women were too old to bear children. Hang them, they figured and let the living know that the Devils meant business.

"Where did you get the gun?"

"Found it."

"Who put up the trap. The roadblock?"

"We both did," said Bobby.

"Why?"

"Because they might come back," said Emily matter of factly.

"And we wanted to ready for them next time," said Bobby simply.

Bonner looked sadly at Bobby. He had already ceased to be a young kid. The horrors of the last few days had compressed a lifetime of experience into a few days. He had cried when Bonner found them but those would probably be the last tears he would ever cry. Bobby had left his childhood behind in a ruined village. Now he was started on the road to becoming a man. And a killer.

Chapter Seven

Bonner didn't sleep much that night. He settled the kids down, placing them close to the fire and wrapping them in the blankets that he and the Mean Brothers usually used. Then he sat between them on the hard ground, a huddled figure curled on either side of him, his back resting against the hard frame of his tough machine. The kids fell asleep almost as soon as they lay down although Bonner could sense their eyes on him, studying him in those few minutes between sleep and waking. They stared, their eyes glinting in the orange light as if to reassure themselves that he was really there, that he wasn't going to leave. Once they decided he was there and there for good, they slept.

It was the sound sleep of security and trust. They let sleep claim them because they knew that Bonner and his silent friends were a powerful bulwark against the horrors of the night and the world it enclosed in the black air. Their instinct told them that Bonner and the Mean Brothers would summon the Furies to protect them, that the three men would destroy all that tried to do them harm.

The Means slept too. Usually one of them would take first watch, awakening Bonner in the night to have him take his turn. But not tonight. They had seen that look on Bonner's face before. He would be awake for a long time. If he needed them all he had to do was wake them.

Usually the stern planes of Bonner's face were closed, granite hard, revealing none of his thoughts. But on nights like this, when he was unobserved by only his two mute partners, his graven features dissolved in the intensity of his thoughts and his face revealed that he was a troubled man.

He was not thinking of the road ahead of him. The Devils that had sliced up Almost Natural were not much on his mind. They were, for all intents and purposes, dead men; they breathed now but they were marked. The manner of their killing Bonner would leave to circumstance. Right now his mind strayed to the two children sleeping by his side. Where could they go? Where could he take them where they would be safe?

No one knew better than Bonner what kind of world it was. There was a law: the law of the gun. If law was sacred, then the gun was the holy relic. You lived, you died, the gun was always triumphant. Force had no conscience—it used men, rather than the other way around. Force, violence, blood, death, those were the wellsprings of the life of the new world. There was no safe place now. To live was to know that life could be taken from you at any moment for any reason by any man who cared to try. Where, Bonner wondered, was there a place for children in all this?

Ahead of him were miles of struggle and he knew he was equal to it. The Mean Brothers—hell, he thought, they would enjoy it. But two kids? How could they endure the horrors that were to come? But where could he leave them in safety? The last safe place on the continent had died a painful death five nights before. He would have to take them with him.

It was a terrible paradox: the safest place, and yet again, the most dangerous, was right by Bonner's side.

In the gray light of dawn the little camp awoke. The Means kicked the dying embers of the fire into something approaching a blaze. They managed to cook a sort of oatmeal from the course cereal they kept in a dirty sack. The mush was tasteless so they put a lot of salt in it—if there was no salt, gunpowder would do—but it was hot at least. It didn't taste like much and it didn't look too good but the warmth made everyone feel better on a damp morning.

Bonner woke the kids gently but Emily still opened her eyes with a start and a cry as if she expected to wake up to find that their rescue had been nothing but a dream.

The Mean Brothers slapped a pile of gray mush onto tin plates and handed them to the kids. Bobby and Emily eyed them curiously and seemed to eat more to avoid offending the Mean Brothers than out of hunger. Bonner remembered the breakfasts that Martha used to put out in the old days: eggs, butter, bread—real food for people who had worked hard to produce it. Bonner always felt guilty eating it. A meal at Martha and Charlie's table would have been the kind of fare that Bonner's fellow smugglers and riders would have killed over. The butter they forced him to slather onto his bread was worth a small fortune—but they gave it away.

The Mean Brothers broke camp, stowing the meager equipment under the seats of Bonner's car. The kids watched, apprehensively, like animals ready to run.

"Are you leaving?" said Bobby.

"We all are. You too," said Bonner.

Relief washed across the kids faces. "Where are we going?" asked Emily.

"We're going to look for your mom and dad."

"Great!" said Bobby.

Bonner squatted down next to them. "Look," he said, "there are some things you should know . . . I want you to understand. Finding your folks is not going to be easy. You're going to see a lot of bad things."

"Fighting, you mean?" asked Bobby.

"Yeah. People are going to get hurt. But, you see, I can't figure out a where there's a safe place to put you."

"We want to come with you," said Emily, brushing a strand of hair from her eyes.

That settled it.

It was a tight squeeze in Bonner's car. Bobby and Emily sat in the laps of the Mean Brothers as if they were huge hairy armchairs. By the time the morning sun etched long shadows in the dew Bonner had put his small party on the road.

He continued to follow the Devils' tracks down the long dirt road until it joined up with a ribbon of old two-lane blacktop at the bottom of the mountain. The road curved away down the valley and without hesitation Bonner pushed his machine out onto it heading south. The tracks were gone, of course, but the Devils would have headed south. Bonner had no doubt there was a fork in the road somewhere up ahead and then he would have to make a decision as to which way they went. Right now, though, he was sure.

The road was littered with the rusty tattered wrecks of tractors and pickups. This had been farm country once. Bonner always made a point of reading the fading signs on the sides of the roads he traveled. The stores more or less made sense to him (Sam's Feed Lot) but others puzzled him (Bob's Big Boy). The large, tall, rectangular boards that didn't appear to be attached to any store or ruin of one that Bonner could see made less sense: FIFTY-FIVE: IT'S THE LAW. RISEN CHIRST IS KING. E-Z LISTENING. 104.2 KHJB CATLINBURG.

It seemed to be some sort of way that the men of the old world communicated with each other while they shot down their nice open roads. The significance of these monster signs was gone for good. When Bobby asked him about one—T.V. 28 BRINGS BACK THE GOOD OLD DAYS then followed by the word M*A*S*H—Bonner could only shrug. There was a lot about the old world he didn't know, things he would never know.

They flashed by a huge sixteen-wheel truck. It lay on its side, the rims of its wheels shorn of tires sticking straight up at the leaden sky. It looked like some enormous stiff dead animal. An angry tear in the rusty sides showed the cargo that the truck had carried once: inside were hundreds of crates crammed full of little skeletons. Chickens. The bones spilled out onto the road and they crunched under Bonner's fat tires.

In this new age, Bonner thought, that many chickens would have made a man rich for life. It would have also made him a target. He would have had to spend half his money and all of his time with his bodyguards—and there was no guarantee that they wouldn't try to knock him off one dark night. Getting yourself killed for chickens. That was the kind of world it was.

The kids stared around them, not quite able to believe what they saw.

"You never came down off the hill, did you?" yelled Bonner over the roar of the engine and the scream of the wind.

Bobby shook his head. "Dad said it was bad down here."

Dad was right, thought Bonner. He knew, of course, that this little corner of dead America was nothing, of course. Here the land had died because the country as a whole had died. Bonner could tell that the bombs had not rained down here bringing their terrible messages of death to this quiet land. But after the bomb places like this had just fallen apart. Perhaps they had fallen prey to fear and hate, when old tribal loathings had come to the surface and ancient scores were settled under the cover of being cut off and the chaos of the world outside. Maybe these little towns had just . . . died.

To the kids it was a world they never knew existed. But Bonner knew they were in for worse shocks. He had seen places where the earth had been torn apart like old rags, where whole cities had been reduced to ash, where the streets were filled with broken glass as deep as snow after a blizzard. But Bobby and Emily had seen their own little piece of horror, worse really than the quiet tombs of the millions of dead, faceless strangers.

Later in the day they saw a touch more of the cruelty that men can work. Lying across the road was a body, a fresh one. Bonner slowed down and pulled up a few yards from the bloody mass.

"Stay here," he said quietly to the kids. He walked up to the corpse and saw that it was a woman. She was lying face down on the hard road surface. Her blond hair swirled out from her head and it was stiff with blood. You didn't have to be an expert to see that she had been beaten to death. Gently, as if she was still alive, Bonner turned her over. Crushed under her body was a tiny corpse of a baby, a complicated tangle of veins and flesh connecting it to his mother's body.

"Mrs. Conners," said Bobby's voice behind him. "She was going to have a baby. Mom said it could come any day. . . ."

Bonner looked at the broken bodies below him and imagined what had happened. The woman had gone into labor on the road. The Devils had refused to stop. She collapsed. The baby was born dead. The woman was too weak to rise. They beat her to death. Usually, pregnant women were prized by slavers. They called them "two-fers." Two for the price of one. These Devils must be in a hurry.

Bobby and his sister looked at the dead woman and her child with that peculiarly distant look that comes into the eyes of those used to observing suffering. Bonner had seen the same look on the faces of riders and Stormers and slaves. He was amazed that the two kids had adopted that kind of reserve so quickly. They were learning—and a piece of them, their innocence, was dying.

A Mean Brother drifted up to Bonner's side. The man giant held his shovel in his hands. He held it inquiringly in front of him. Bonner often buried the victims of random violence he found along the road.

"Yeah," muttered Bonner. "Let's give her a decent burial."

The Mean Brother heard his order and wandered to the side of the road and began burrowing in the hard ground.

Bonner looked down the road. Another innocent person had died, two if you included the baby. Another bloodied corpse: it was a signpost pointing the way towards revenge.

Chapter Eight

By midafternoon mother and child had been carefully laid in the ground. Bonner felt sad that the burial had to be so mean. He had nothing to use as a shroud and not being an eloquent man he could think of no meaningful words to pronounce over her grave. He had to content himself with a silent promise of vengeance—but he knew that meant nothing to the souls that had once occupied the broken bodies now resting in the cold ground. Revenge was something that only satisfied the living.

One of the Mean Brothers heard it first. Bonner was standing over the newly turned earth and the sound didn't quite register in his thoughts. One of the Means tapped him on the shoulder and Bonner tore himself from his melancholy meditations and listened.

Far off, down the road they had already traveled,

came the sounds of what sounded like a huge swarm of motorized hornets. The screaming of engines split the afternoon sky—it grew louder with the passing of every second. The engines that produced the banshee wail were small and running hot. Even the kids could tell that they were not sounds produced by deep-booming Harley pan- and knuckleheads or big cylinder machines like Bonner's. The wild whine shattered the air. The kids looked bewildered and tense as if poised, ready to run. The Means looked down the road then over at Bonner. If he said "danger" they were ready to stand and fight.

A slight smile played on Bonner's face. "Don't worry kids," he said. "There's only one pack of riders that makes a racket like that. And they're on our side." Or, thought Bonner, most of the time they are.

"Who are they?" asked Emily.

"You'll see." He turned to the Mean Brothers. "We're going to have a little company." And Bonner had to admit to himself that he was glad of it. The visitors were a very tough set of bring downs, probably some of the toughest, meanest riders on the road. If they chose to come along after the slave column Bonner would be glad to have them.

One of the Mean Brothers was looking enquiringly at Bonner, as if to say "who?"

"They're called the Lash," said Bonner.

A second or two later the first bikes wailed into view. A moment later there were two dozen more. A second after that they had screeched to a halt around Bonner and his odd party. The Mean Brothers and the kids stared at their visitors and the visitors stared back. It was hard to say who was more surprised.

Not one of the two dozen riders was over four feet tall. That weird convention of bikers that had come down the road so suddenly was made up exclusively of midgets and dwarves, probably every last surviving miniature human on the continent rode with the Lash.

The bikes they rode were old scooters and boonie bikes, light, low-capacity machines that wouldn't have carried a full grown man too fast anywhere. But the light members of the Lash got hold of them and chopped them down and souped them up and made sure that they moved like mosquitoes on the highway. The Lashmen were experts with their little machines and they knew every secret for getting every ounce of power, for pulling each extra sliver of power from their hot little engines.

Every rider wore a couple of weapons. Big Browning, Winchester, and Marlin rifles, most taller than their owners, were slung over their broad, squat backs. Mammoth Smith and Wesson and Colt handguns were strapped to their thick, misshappen thighs. Bowie knives were stuck into belts and machetes trailed between their legs like tails.

They were grizzled, dirty, wrinkled, mean small men. Bonner had known some full-sized riders who had made the mistake of thinking that the Lashmen's small size meant that they were easy marks. Those guys were dead now. They died without really ever figuring out what hit them. The Lash had a motto and they stuck to it: "Fuck with us and we'll kill you." It wasn't exactly eloquent but it was true.

"I seen that big rig of yours two miles off," said the tallest of the Lash. "Knew it was you right off. And a good thing too or me and the boys would have come in blasting, Bonner."

"I'm glad of that," said Bonner. The little guy who had spoken was obviously the leader. He rode an old Vespa scooter with the wigs sheared off and with two exhaust pipes swept up behind him high above his red-fuzz-covered head. He jumped off his perch and rested two knotty fists on his hips. He looked coolly at Bonner who towered over him. There were two long barreled weapons on his back. One was some kind of over-and-under shotgun that looked like it was about two hundred years old and a nice old Winchester lever action.

"So how you doing, Floyd," asked Bonner, reaching down to take the leader's hand.

"Shit," said Floyd in his gravelly voice. He paused and hocked about half a pint of slime onto a broken roadbed. "Shit. Just shit, man. Same old shit. Shit, shit, shit, shit. You know."

Bonner smiled. "Know all about it, Floyd."

"Who the fuck are the mountains?" demanded Floyd, looking at the Mean Brothers—although given the size of Floyd he could have been referring to Bobby and Emily who were tall for their age.

"Mean Brothers," said Bonner, "I want you to meet Floyd and his riders, known as the Lash of the Little People. And that's Bobby and Emily, friends of mine . . ."

"Kids? You traveling with kids? What kind of pecker-brained idea is that?"

"We're looking for their mother and father," said Bonner.

"You gettin' as soft as a fuckin' pimp," said Floyd spitting again.

Emily was beaming at the tiny men that were spread out around her. "They're so cute," she said delightedly. "I want to pick one up."

Floyd spun on his heel. The red fur on his ears and head seemed to stand up in anger. His pale blue eyes blazed. He strode over to the girl and fixed his angry glare at her.

"Okay bitch, listen up. We ain't cute, we ain't funny. We ain't no motherfuckin' elfs and we ain't no fuckin' fairies. We ain't little kids, we ain't tiny-teeny little fuckin' happy little guys who sing stupid fuckin' little songs. We are about the meanest fuckin' pack of riders this side of radlep territory. Got it?"

"Sorry," said Emily and giggled behind her hand.

"Don't be tough on the kids," said Bonner.

"Good fucking thing they're with you or I would have blasted her in half."

"They don't mean no harm," said Bonner.

"Piss me off," said Floyd.

The Lashmen had all dismounted. Some were stretching after their long ride, others had wandered off the road to relieve themselves. A few clustered around the Mean Brothers and were looking up at them as if the Brothers were two great, tall trees.

One of the Lashmen looked deep into the Mean Brother eyes and then announced with a sneer:

"You're not so fucking tough," then he spat at the Mean Brothers.

The Mean regarded him for a moment then reached down to grab the little guy's shirtfront. Out of the corner of his eye Bonner saw the Mean stoop to snatch up the midget.

"Hold it," shouted Bonner. The Mean froze midway towards the little man. Bonner knew the way of the Lash very well. They didn't like to be picked up and thrown around like dolls. They saw that kind of behavior as an attack—and an attack on one of the Lash was construed as an attack on all. The Mean Brother, of course, could have minced the midget in his hairy hands but he wouldn't have been able to withstand the concentrated firepower of two-dozen-odd guns fired all at once.

Bonner knew that the Mean had no intention of hurting the small man but the other Lashmembers didn't know that.

"These are friends," explained Bonner. "They don't mean no trouble."

The Mean Brother shrugged, as if to say, "I didn't mean no trouble."

"Fuck you," screamed the dwarf who had challenged the Mean, "I don't need your help, Bonner."

"Shut your fucking yap," rapped Floyd. It seemed that Floyd alone could keep the little dervishes in hand.

A crook-backed midget, perhaps the ugliest of the bunch, although he did have considerable competition, crab-walked up to Emily. He tried to arrange his squashed features into something approaching an ingratiating smile. He succeeded only in displaying a not very appetizing collection of very black teeth.

"Hi," said the tiny man.

"Hi," said Emily, looking down as if from a great height.

"You can pick me up if ya wanna," he said.

"No, the other man said . . ."

"Pay no attention to Floyd. He's just a dick. You are one pretty little doll."

He was Emily's first suitor and she blushed. She stiffened when he placed a callused hand on her soft pink knee.

"Don't," she said.

"C'mon girlie, lets just the two of us go for a little walk. I could really go for you . . ."

"Rufus," barked Floyd.

Rufus withdrew his hand from Emily's knee as if her leg had suddenly turned red-hot.

"What?"

"Don't fuck with the little pussy."

Rufus slunk off, casting, as he went, lust-filled glances in Emily's direction.

"That little fuck is a cunt hound," said Floyd to Bonner.

"I'll leave it to you to keep him away from her." It was always wise to let the Lashmen police each other. "But I tell you, if he bothers her . . ."

"Calm down, Bonner. I'll see that Rufus don't bother your little puppy. I can't stand the shit . . . Besides, what makes you think that we're gonna be around that long?"

"Thought there might be a chance that we would ride together."

"You got a target in mind?"

"You heard of Almost Normal?"

"Heard of it," said Floyd, "never been there."

"And you never will," said Bonner flatly. "It's gone. A bunch of slavers took it down a couple of days ago."

"What kinda slavers."

"I figure Devils. They took just about everybody in the town. They took the kids' mother and father . . . Friends of mine."

"So they fucked with your friends and you are going to fuck with them, right?"

"Something like that."

"What's in it for us?"

"You heard of Farkas?"

"Yep."

"Anything you can find on his farm, it's yours."

"You mean you want to attack Farkas' slave farm?"

"Yes. That's exactly what I want to do. Unless I can get to the column before they are inside it."

"What makes you think Farkas is behind the raid on the Normal place?"

"They were Devils. They ran in a big force. They're headed south. It all adds up to Farkas. . . ."

"Farkas got some tough shit Devils around his place."

Bonner knew when it was time to launch a compliment and he tempered this one with a heavy dose of greed. "Tougher than the Lash? And if he has a lot of guns around, it stands to reason that he's got a lot to protect. Farkas is one of the richest guys around. I'm willing to give you anything he has," Bonner added with a grin.

"Still pretty tough," said Floyd.

"Maybe not." Bonner stirred the dust at his feet.

"You got a plan?"

"Not a plan exactly, an idea."

"What kind of idea."

"You ever heard of Farkas being hit?"

"Nope."

"Then he's probably not expecting it, is he?"

"Pra'bly not."

"The Lash might be able to give him a little trouble then, wouldn't you say?"

Floyd laughed. "Bonner, trouble is our business."

"So we ride together?"

"I'll ask the boys. They always have a say, you know?"

"Yeah," Bonner said, "I know." He also knew that the Lash would do anything Floyd told them to.

"What happens if we catch your friends in the column before they get to Farkas' place?"

"Then you have your choice," said Bonner.

"Choice of what?"

"We can hit Farkas' anyway. The deal stands. I'll help but the stuff is yours. Or . . ."

"Or . . ."

"Or I'll owe you one."

Floyd was impressed. Bonner never owed a man anything. But if he said he'd be there sometime in the future when the Lash needed him, Floyd knew that he meant it. It was common knowledge amongst the riders that Bonner always kept his word.

Chapter Nine

Floyd circulated Bonner's idea among his men and found—as he suspected he would—that the Lash of the Little People went for it in a big way. Farkas was an almost mythical figure in the minds of virtually every rider on the continent. Few people had ever seen him—but everyone had heard of him. They said that he had carved himself a rich little principality on the eastern edge of Berger's Hotstates. He paid some kind of rent to Berger and in return Berger let him use as many Devils—skag and silk—as he needed. Farkas was also said to have his own private army and some people said that it was a measure of his won strength that Berger would rather make peace with Farkas than to fight him.

There was no doubt that Farkas was a big source of revenue for Berger. Farkas' was a flourishing industry—Berger always said that no one had a touch with slave rearing like Farkas. His product was much in demand and Farkas tended his human garden like the most conscientious gardener.

But most important of all, to the Lash anyway, was the simple fact that Farkas was rich. They said that he was as rich as Berger and Carey, maybe as rich as Leatherman. That his riches were heavily defended made him that much more interesting.

The Lashmen stood around Floyd listening to his plan and, for the most part agreeing. Only Rufus scowled, but he always looked pissed off. It was no secret that he thought he ought to be in command.

"We hit this slave column Bonner's heard about first," announced Floyd.

"What the fuck for?" demanded Rufus.

" 'Cause that's the deal," said Floyd patiently.

"The deal with who?" Rufus insisted, acting as if he hadn't been listening.

"With Bonner."

"We don't need him."

"Rufus," said Floyd, "you ever seen him fight?"

"Nope."

"Then shut the fuck up. We need him."

"Trouble with you, Floydie," said Rufus, "is that you just can't resist the tall fucks in this world. It's as if you're ashamed of what you is."

Floyd colored red to the tips of his ears and marched over to where Rufus stood. He grabbed him by the shoulders.

"How about I beat your fuckin' face in?"

Rufus stared back. "Like to see you try, you little prick."

"This don't seem to me to be the way to start a big raid," said a wrinkled Lashman known, for no known reason, as Bunny.

"Yeah," put in another gang member, this one called Sammy, "let it ride you guys."

Floyd let go of Rufus and lowered his fist.

"Okay," he said as he ostentatiously turned his back on Rufus, "you guys listen to me. Anytime one of you thinks they can run this outfit better than me, all you gotta do is let me know . . ." He rested his hand on the gun strapped to his thick thigh. ". . . And we'll talk about it." The crowd was silent.

Then Bunny spoke. "I don't think we got any problems with you leadin' the Lash, Floyd." The rest of the gang—except Rufus—murmured their agreement.

Floyd smiled. "Good." Then he whipped around and smacked his fist into Rufus' jaw. Rufus was so surprised all he could do was fall down.

"Don't call me a prick," said Floyd as he stood over him, "again."

Scouts went out ahead of the riders to see what they could find. Bonner and the main force followed. It might be a couple of days before they located them, but Bonner had no doubt that they would find them eventually.

THE OUTRIDER

The scouts were back in a day or so and they had located their quarry.

"It's a hell of a thing," said one of them, "we snuck up on them late yesterday afternoon and we figured they had put up for the night. You know, making camp."

"We waited," said his companion, wiping some road grime from his brow, "figurin' we'd follow them the next morning, ya know?"

"But the fuckers didn't move. They sat there all fuckin' day. Weird."

"There's a lot of 'em?" asked Floyd.

"Fifty maybe. And the slaves."

"Devils, right?" asked Bonner.

"Yep."

"Skag or silk?"

"A lotta silk, some skaggies taking care of the slaves."

"Man, *are* they silk, too. I mean, these guys look like they got the best of everything. I mean, these guys are Berger's top silkies. Big Harleys, all of 'em got automatic weapons. Sure are pretty . . ."

"And they're just sittin' there?" asked Floyd.

"Jes' sittin.'"

Floyd turned to Bonner. "What do you think?"

"I think we ought to take a look."

Bonner and the Lash moved out. The gang screamed onto the road, their engine wailing as if they couldn't wait to carry their vicious little riders to battle. The deeper, steadier boom of Bonner's big engine set up a menacing counterpoint to the high-pitched whine of the Lashmen's little bikes. The combined sounds would have made a tough man pale a little if he heard them coming at him.

Bobby and Emily had never ridden in formation before and the swirl of engine noise around them made them a little scared, yet also seemed to exhilarate them. It was as if the sea of sound was proof that they were safe. Looking at Bonner guiding his force and the tiny little killers hunched over the handlebars of their machines it seemed to the kids that no one could prevail against such a powerful force.

Bonner was not so sure. The fact that the slave column had paused on the road meant something. It could be something simple as mechanical trouble— maybe a couple of the big trucks had broken down at the same time and they couldn't transport their cargo of doomed men and women. But the scouts had seen no sign of work being done on the vehicles that slavers called "meat wagons."

Bonner had a feeling that the slavers were waiting for something. He hoped it wasn't reinforcements. The Lash was outnumbered as it was. Not seriously, it was only about two to one. Bonner had no doubt that a determined group of Lashmen could take out a big force of silk Devils. The Devils were good but they weren't Stormers and they certainly weren't Radleps. Bonner had seen the Lash slice up a lot of Stormers in his time. When the little guys started fighting they were something to behold.

They stopped a mile or two short of the Devil camp and the scouts were sent out again to make sure that the prey was still camped where they had left them. They reported back within an hour.

"Still there," announced one.

"They're havin' a party. They got a big fire goin' and they're drinkin. They got a couple of the slave women out an', ya know."

"A party," said Floyd. "And we wasn't invited. Those fucks hurt my feelings."

Bonner nodded. A party was good news. If they were lucky, the Devils would be good and drunk.

"I say take them now," said the Outrider tersely.

"Fuck yeah," said Floyd with a grin.

Skippy, the leader of the Devil battalion had his outfit's motto tattooed on his forehead. ("You're Dead Sucker.") The letters were blue and clumsily etched onto his forehead. Since he had had it done some years before, it had begun to itch. He scratched his forehead and listened to the buzzing in his ears. He had had a lot to drink because he and his men were sick to death of waiting. They were bored so they decided to have a party.

Then it hit Skippy. That wasn't drink thrumming through his head. It was the sound of engines.

"Hey, shithead," he shouted at his much despised lieutenant, a Silk Devil called Johnny. Johnny was sitting on the ground, a bottle of the Devil brew, usually called "Gut" resting on his knee. He was watching two of his fellow Devils tearing the clothes off a screaming slave woman. She was about seventeen.

"Hey shithead," reiterated Skippy.

"What?" said Johnny, refusing to take his eyes off the struggling woman. The two Devils had shredded the upper portion of her dress and her white breasts were exposed to the warm afternoon sunshine. One of her ravishers slapped her hard on the cheek. Tears streamed from her eyes.

"They're here."

"Great."

"Well, you assholes gonna be lying around blind drunk when our fuckin' honored guests show up?"

"Fuck 'em."

A few Devils were looking toward the horizon. Their long wait was over. "Now we can get the fuck out of here," said one.

Bonner was the first over the crest. The Devil camp was spread out on an old piece of asphalt a couple of acres across. Bonner had seen sites like this all over the continent and he had never figured out just what they were for. The tarmac was not laid flat like in a parking lot. It was a vast expanse of cracked black paving with rhythmically placed waves, humps, spaced from one end of the piece to the other. In the center of the dark patch of paving was always a square low building. The whole park was scattered about with poles rising to just below chest height. The whole setup faced a big white board, a huge expanse of plaster that seemed to be eighty or a hundred feet high by about forty feet across. Usually they were blank, but on this one someone had painted, in big red, angry letters, GOD, WHY DID YOU FORSAKE US?

There was a smaller sign on the access road that Bonner led the Lash men down? STAR-LITE DRIVE IN. OSED FO E SEASO. Drive into what, Bonner wondered.

In this case, a firefight.

Chapter Ten

"Means," bellowed Bonner, "take care of the kids!" He whipped out his Hi Standard and blasted a slug into the drunk, startled body of a Devil who was just standing there watching the murderous cavalcade of midgets sweeping into the camp like a stream that suddenly overran its banks.

Skippy dived for his gun. "Holy shit!" he said, "it's those crazy little fuckers and . . ." He didn't want to say Bonner's name out loud in case by not saying it he could make the man go away.

A chatter of bullets poured over Bonner's shoulder as all the Lashmen started up, firing from the saddles of their tiny machines. A couple of Devils fell. The tiny bikes screamed around the bumpy acreage, rushing up and over the humps then littered the park. The bikes were airborne for the second after they left the crest, then they slapped down onto the tarmac and ascended the next.

Floyd got a bead on a fleeing Devil and chased him across the broken asphalt. The midget stood up on the little running board of his scooter and lined up the spot between the shoulder blade of the running Devil. The big Dan Wesson pistol barked and the slug seemed to explode on the spine of the Devil. Instantly, the man's shoulders and neck turned into a bloody hash. He fell and for the hell of it, Floyd ran his scooter over the bloody body, the studded tires tearing up the tattered flesh.

"Fuckin' pansy," screamed Floyd over his shoulder.

The Devils, all of a sudden pretty sober, were running around, fumbling for weapons. A lucky shot from one of them tore into the throat of a Lashmen and the tiny body fell from the saddle. Bunny saw his brother little guy fall and started after his killer. An inarticulate cry of rage broke from his lips.

The killer flopped to his belly and started laying down fire ahead of him, unaware that Bunny had marked him for death. The midget screeched to a halt next to the big Devil and leaped from his bike right onto the back of the wildly firing tough guy. Heels out, Bunny landed with the combined force of his weight and his rage on the Devil. On impact he splintered a half a dozen small bones in the Devil's back. The Devil rolled to one side.

"Get the fuck off me," he screamed through his pain.

"Dick," yelled Bunny and his Colt spat six hot shots into the silk's face.

The Mean Brothers were quite unhappy with their assignment. Bonner had stopped the car and had picked up his Steyr and slipped his cut down shotgun from its nest and was now sprinting across the broken tarmac, the battle raging around him. The Mean Brothers didn't know where he was going, but they watched him enviously. But an order from Bonner was an order they would never disobey. They pulled Bobby and Emily from the back of the war wagon and hunkered them down in the lee of the heavy machine. They shielded the kids with their giant forms. Bonner said to take care of the kids and to the Mean Brothers that meant stopping a stray bullet with their bodies if they had to. But they felt cheated.

Bobby and Emily poked their heads out from the hairy protecting arms and watched wide eyed.

The Devils had gotten over their initial shock and they were taking advantage of the cover provided by the trucks, and the hummocky ground to repel the invaders. Skippy and Johnny were lying side by side and firing at the speeding Lashmen. They took down two apiece and thought they were pretty hot shit for doing so. That was before Floyd blasted their heads into pink gray pulps with his shotgun.

One of the Silks, a man called Willy, had some pretensions to brains. He figured out instantly why the Outrider was here and he moved to use that information against him. Willy knew that Bonner was there to rescue the slaves. That was the kind of stupid gallantry that people like Willy couldn't understand. Right now, Willy wasn't going to try and figure out the Outrider's motives; all he knew was the slaves were his tickets out of a sudden and painful death at the hands of Bonner and the Lashmen.

Willy squirmed across the hot asphalt towards the little hut that most of the slaves were huddled in. Willy hoped with all his soul that no one noticed him as he made his way slowly towards the brokendown shack.

He needn't have worried. A number of the Devils had recovered from the shock of the sudden attack and were doing their best to drive off their vicious attackers. Willy figured that was what made him smart and the others dumb. They were busy fighting and he was busy escaping. The Lashmen were still buzzing around the drive in like angry hornets. They moved too fast for most of the Devils to get a line on them and the little men were expert fighters from the saddle. Rarely did a shot miss.

Floyd was having fun, running a Devil ragged all over the broken paving. Instead of cutting the big man down with a single well-placed shot, he chased him, staying on the Devil's tail, chasing the hard guy all over the place. He circled and buzzed and rushed like a sheep dog corraling a wandering animal. The Devil was panting from the exertion and, instead of standing his ground and fighting he kept running—which was just what Floyd wanted. The midget leader reached behind him and yanked a yard-long machete from his saddlebag which he waved over his head, screaming:

"Take a look, you big fuck! Take a look!"

The Devil tossed a quick look over his shoulder and saw what he must have thought was a vision from Hell. A tiny man with a scraggly beard mounted on a weird machine, his green eyes glowing, his voice raised in an unnatural screech waving a few feet of sharp metal that he seemed to be very anxious to drive deep into the Devil's body. In the second that the Devil glanced over his shoulder he ran full tilt into one of the metal poles that were dotted around the park. He cracked his head painfully on the heavy pipe and mashed his balls against the unforgiving steel. He slumped to the ground and was just conscious enough to register that the midget was upon him.

As the scooter roared by him the little man reared in his seat and swept the shining blade down with sickening force. The blade slit the Devil's skull, opening it wide to the bright morning.

An incoherent scream of joy and rage broke from Floyd's lips. He was especially delighted because the Devil he had just killed must have been six six if he was an inch.

Willy kicked in the door of the hut that sheltered the slaves, took a step into the room, and got cracked on the head by a chair.

The men and women of Almost Normal were not used to being slaves and didn't know that they were supposed to cower in terror when one of their captors chose to come near them. Amos, the slave that had belted Willy wasn't going to sit there and get murdered by some tough guy—at least, he wasn't going to get killed without a fight.

"Fuck," screamed Willy from the ground where he lay. Amos was about to pounce on him and start beating him with his powerful fists but courage was no match for lead. The revolver in Willy's hand spoke loud and Amos' strong face opened up, a bloody mass of bone and brain. He dropped.

Willy was on his feet in a second. "Okay," he screamed brandishing the pistol, keeping the unarmed men back. "We're leaving . . ."

Willy left the hut surrounded by a few of the slave women. He walked in the center of them, his ancient Colt held against the temple of one of them. Bonner was too sentimental to chance a shot at him.

"Everybody keep close to me," he hissed at the women. "We are headed for that bike over there." He gestured towards the big 1200 that was parked a distance away. He planned to get right next to it, gun it to life, and get the hell out of there. He chanced a shot in the back as he fled but he figured it was worth it. If he was on his powerful bike he might hightail it out of there. To stay was to die.

The firefight crackled around him. He and his hostages inched their way towards the bike.

Bonner saw them. Willy saw Bonner. "Stay back, man," screamed Willy, "stay back."

Bonner stood tall. Willy was almost completely covered by the bodies of the slaves. A tiny sliver of his head showed from behind the long hair of the women who quivered under the press of the gun to her temple.

Bonner saw the slaves. He saw Willy—he saw enough of Willy to chance a shot. Bonner didn't think. He was caught in the whirling wind of fury that turned him from an ordinary man with ordinary powers into that most feared of all men: the man with a mission, the man with righteousness on his side. He raised his Hi Standard and instinct did the rest. Bonner's eyes closed on the few inches of Willy's head that he could see. In that second there was nothing else on earth, no other target for the Outrider's gun.

It all happened so fast that Willy didn't register that Bonner had fired at him until he was sitting on the ground looking at his ear which had been torn from his head by the steel-jacketed slug that winged him. Blood as forceful as a fountain spurted from the side of his head and drenched the tarmac.

Like the opening of a flower, the female slaves had fallen away from him and he was sitting on the ground unprotected, his Colt in his hand. He looked up, exposing his dirty neck. The Hi Standard barked again and tore his throat out.

The Mean Brothers had seen the whole thing. They exchanged glances. That, they said, was shooting.

Bobby too, had seen the Outrider cut down Willy and his heart swelled with admiration and pride. But he had seen something else: the woman that had shielded Willy was his mother. She was gray and thin and so scared that she hadn't even registered that her saviour had been her old friend Bonner.

But Bobby had seen her and he decided he was going to finish the job that Bonner had started. He squirmed from the Mean Brother's grasp and dashed for a gun that lay a few yards from the sheltering lee of Bonner's war wagon. The Mean Brother made a quick grasp for the running kid but the shirt tail of the boy just eluded his grasp. The Mean set off after him.

Two midgets had cornered a Devil and were methodically kicking him to death. The big Devil rocked and roared trying to crawl away from the metal-toed boots that the little men slammed into the Devil's flanks. A rib cracked, then another and suddenly the Devil tasted blood in his mouth. One of his sharpened, split ribs had gouged itself deep into the soft sac of his lung. He was going to drown in his own blood. He stared up at his tormentors and thought he was dreaming when he saw one of the little guy's head explode.

A motorized figure rushed by Bonner. The Steyr in his hands chattered of its own accord and sliced the back of the rider to ribbons. The bike skidded off and wrapped itself around one of the poles. The rider fell heavily at Bonner's booted feet. Bonner raised a steel heel and smashed the plastic face mask of his most recent victim. Torn, disfigured dead features stared back at him. The creature spread before him had a face of unparalled hideousness. His lips were a tattered reddish line of flesh; his cheeks were a mangled mass of scars and scabs.

Bonner kicked the helmet off. The thing had no hair, just a crazy patchwork of lesions and sores. Bonner knew instantly what it was: Radlep.

Chapter Eleven

Floyd saw them, too. Radleps, radiation lepers, Leatherman's most feared, most hated, and toughest killers were flooding onto the asphalt battlefield. Floyd and Bonner instantly had the same thought: these were the guys that the Devils had been waiting for. It was some kind of link up between Berger's best and Leatherman's meanest. Neither the Lash Leader nor the Outrider bothered right then to figure out why they were joining forces but suddenly the battle that looked like it was going their way had changed.

Bonner ran a practiced eye over the 'leps that were swarming onto the drive-in court and knew instantly that there were easily a hundred of the killing monsters. It was odds that they couldn't fight.

Floyd was no coward but he knew when it was

time to go. He kicked the engine to life and screamed for the Lash to follow. The midgets were getting pasted by the sudden influx masked slaughterers.

"Bonner," yelled Floyd.

"I know," responded the Outrider. He wouldn't run to save his skin. But if he stayed he would die and that would be the end of the slaves. He sprinted for his car.

"Means! Let's go."

But the Means were gone. Cowering in the shelter of the car was Emily, scared beyond words.

"Where are they?" yelled Bonner.

Emily, her blue eyes streaming with tears, couldn't find her voice.

Bonner turned from her and surveyed the battle field.

Bobby had reached the gun and picking it up had dashed towards his mother only to find his path cut off by the column of Radleps that had come rushing onto the field. He had lived enough life in the past few days to know an enemy when he saw one. The automatic in his hand had spat lead without his thinking about it. He missed the nearest 'lep, but the hot slug found the fuel tank of the bike clutched between the monster's scaly legs. It blew and threw a burning Radlep from the bike.

The thing hit the ground, his body aflame. The pain seared through him but it didn't distract him enough to prevent him from leveling his rifle at Bobby's frail body. The radleps had a rule: Kill the man who brought you down. Bobby fired again into the mass of flaming flesh and tore away a good-sized piece of the radlep's cheek. But still it wasn't enough to take out the horribly dying killing machine.

Bobby's mind seemed to have switched off and his reflexes took over. He gently squeezed the trigger, just the way Bonner had taught him those thousand years ago. He had drawn a bead on the crackling flesh and he knew just where the bullet would hit the burning tough man. But there was no blast and kick from the heavy revolver. He had used all the ammunition that remained in the discarded gun.

The Radlep had him. Or so he thought. Just as he pulled the trigger a Mean Brother landed on the Radlep's back. Both huge feet pounded onto the burning carcass, and the Mean did a little dance there, as if trying to beat out the flames. But he wasn't saving the 'lep from a fiery death. He was pounding the man's spine into the gravel. The flames singed the hair as thick as fur on the man mountain's legs. But he didn't stop there. He reached down and grasped the 'lep by the neck and pulled back, curving the broken body into a warped arc. He felt the satisfying snap and collapse of the backbone.

For good measure the Mean picked up the fire-ravaged corpse and threw it back to the ground. It was dead. It had never fired a shot at the kid. The Mean was pleased with his work. 'Leps were particularly hated by the Mean Brothers.

The other Mean had scooped Bobby in his strong arms and ran with him back to Bonner's car.

"Where's the other one?" bellowed Bonner. The Mean Brother tossed Bobby into the back of the car.

"Where's your brother?" demanded Bonner.

The Mean looked over his shoulder and looked back at the swirling mass of Radleps. His brother was somewhere in the middle of that. He started back towards the battle. But Bonner knew better.

He grabbed the remaining Mean Brother by the arm. "No, Meanie, please . . ."

The Mean Brother shook himself loose. If his brother was in there he was going to get him. He shook himself free from Bonner's grasp.

A 'lep came racing down on them. Bonner blasted him off his cycle with the shotgun that lay on the seat next to him. Then, as if nothing had happened, he turned back to the Mean.

"Don't go. Don't go. I'm telling you . . ." Bonner drew a deep breath. "Meanie, you *owe* me . . ."

The Mean Brother looked over his shoulder again, his big features creased by the agony of his decision. He owed the man. He had sworn to himself that he would always follow him. His brother would be pissed if he knew. . . . He climbed into the car and Bonner slammed it into gear.

A Radlep pursued them across the tarmac, hunched low over the fuel tank of his bike. He fired over the handlebars and the slug buried itself in the retreating dash of Bonner's machine. Bonner glanced at the Mean by his side. The big silent man was watching the 'lep behind him like a cat watching a bird. Bonner could tell what the Mean Brother was thinking: one more, let him get close enough, one more . . .

Bonner stood on his brakes and the 'lep couldn't stop fast enough to prevent a collision. His bike slammed into the rear of Bonner's car and the 'lep flew over his handlebars landing heavily inside the machine.

The Mean Brother and a 'lep take up a lot of room in a small area like that so it seemed to the two kids and to Bonner as if the air was suddenly filled with the flailing limbs of the scarred killer and the hairy giant.

The 'lep that had suddenly dropped in for a visit had a reputation for extraordinary strength in his outfit. What he didn't know was that no matter how strong he was he would never match the blind killing fury of a Mean Brother who has just lost his partner. The Mean Brother was in no mood to play games. He grabbed the 'lep in a lock so tight that three men couldn't have broken it. With his free hand he reached for Bonner's blades. The Outrider shifted slightly in the seat to allow the huge man access. Almost reverently the Mean slid the knife from the holster. He raised it high and it seemed to flash in the morning air. Then it plunged deep into the 'lep's body. It sliced neatly into the 'lep's bony back, severing a host of veins and arteries. Blood welled into the 'lep's lungs and filled his throat. The Mean tightened his grasp on the living corpse's throat and closed it. The blood had nowhere to go save backwards. It filled the 'lep's stomach and then forced itself into his intestines. The 'lep was now a struggling bag of blood. Blood filled his sinuses and poured out of his nose. The knifeblade wiggled in his back.

Then the Mean tossed him over the side, extracting the blade as he tossed him out on the road. The release of the pressure on his neck caused the blood to rush every direction it could.

Emily looked back to see the 'lep retching and coughing an ever-widening pool of gore around his broken body. He thrashed a second or two in the huge lake of his own blood, his broken body frantically searching for a way to staunch the flow of his life's fluid. His clothes grew heavy with his blood. He flopped a second or two more, like a fish out of water, then slopped back down into the pool, his body stained from head to toe with bright red blood. He would bleed for an hour after his soul had arrived in hell.

The battle had been costly for both sides. The Devils never knew what hit them. They had taken casualties that amounted to forty out of their entire force and the Lash had hurt the Radleps bad, too.

But where there had once been two dozen midgets there were now only sixteen. And, of course, the Mean Brother was gone.

Bonner and the Lash had headed as far out of Radlep range as they could get. By nightfall Bonner was sure that they weren't being followed any more and his weary, mauled force stopped for the night.

The Lash bedded down and Floyd went among them to see how they had fared. The little men ate what they could then dropped off to sleep. The battle had drained them. But before they slept they told Floyd what he knew they would say. They wanted revenge. They wanted to take those 'leps and they wanted Farkas. They wanted blood.

Before he slept Floyd spoke to Bonner. "They're mad," he said.

"Look," said Bonner, "I'm sorry. I didn't figure we'd run into 'leps like that."

"The hell with that, Bonner," said Floyd. "Who coulda figured we'd find a bunch of 'leps a way out here? Hey, that was just bad luck."

"The Lash took a lot of bring downs," said Bonner.

"They knew the odds, man, it happens. It ain't the first time we lost riders, ya know."

"I know."

"You gotta figure it was a helluva fight though, man. We nearly skinned them fuckin' Devils. I bet there ain't six without a scratch. That ain't bad, two to one, you know what I mean?"

"I know," said Bonner again.

"An lemme tell you something else, those boys of mine, they want to try again. They want to kill like I never seen 'em before. So if you think this ride is over, you are one crazy fucking tall person."

"Count me in," said Bonner.

"What? You think I counted you out?"

"Nope."

"I'll tell you, Bonner man, there's so much hate out there"—he gestured towards the sleeping mounds of Lashmen—"man, they are so mad, you could get a tan off 'em."

Bobby felt bad. He crept over to the remaining Mean Brother and tried to say what was on his mind. "I'm sorry . . ." The kid was close to tears. "I'm sorry . . . If I hadn't run off, well, your brother would be here now. . . ."

The Mean shrugged. He was doing what he was told, he tried to say. Bonner said take care of the kids and so he took care of them. He did what he had to do. No hard feelings, kid. The Mean reached out with a hairy arm and draped it over Bobby's shoulders. If he's dead, he died the way he wanted to. . . .

But it didn't make Bobby feel any better.

And it didn't help the Mean Brother any. He hoped his brother was alive, but he doubted it. A Mean Brother went down swinging against his enemies—he didn't surrender. The Mean waited until everyone was asleep, then he wandered away from the camp a ways. Then, sure that no one could see him, he allowed big, salty tears to stain his dirty face. Then, staring at the moon he swore revenge.

Chapter Twelve

A cloud of blue smoke and the acrid smell of cordite hung over the battlefield. The twisted, broken bodies of the fallen lay strewn about in awkward tangles of limbs and spilled guts. Their unnatural poses attested to the sudden violence of their deaths. A few, faint cries of the dying drifted up to join the pall that hung above them.

The 'leps had dismounted and their leader, a hideous burn victim called Roy stood in the center of it all looking around him. Most of the bodies were Devils. There were a few Lashmen. There were too many Radleps, and that annoyed him.

A Devil whimpered and crawled a few feet across the pavement.

"Jackson," rasped Roy, pointing at the bleeding Devil, "take care of him. Take care of 'em all."

The 'lep nodded and casually pumped a slug into the wounded Devil's head. The Devil stopped moving. Jackson wandered from body to body and kicked each one. The few that he found still alive, he killed.

The Devils that had survived watched glassy-eyed. They stood around, looking slightly disoriented, like the survivors of some huge natural disaster. Roy walked over to one of them.

"Who's in command?"

"Huh?" said the Devil.

"Who's in charge of this unit?"

The Devil stared back at the burn victim as if the 'lep was speaking in a foreign language.

"The man is talking to you," said a 'lep who was standing nearby.

"Who's your commander?"

"Oh," said the Devil, as if the words suddenly made sense. "Him," he said, pointing to the mushed-up corpse of Skippy.

"Okay," said the 'lep, "you're commanding the Devils now."

"Oh," said the Devil, "okay."

"Get your men together—" Roy gestured at the Devils who were standing around "—and organize the slaves. We're moving out."

One Devil managed to recover his senses faster than the rest. "Now ain't that just like a fuckin' freak Radlep," he said nastily. "You walk in here like you own the place and start giving orders. No sir, I ain't no doom freak burn victim. I don't take orders from no fuckin' 'leps. Got it?''

"Yeah," said Roy, turning his glittering lizard eyes on him. "I got it." Then Roy turned to Jackson. "Shoot him."

"Huh?" said the Devil. There was a crack from the big handgun that Jackson carried and a piece of the Devil's skull spiralled away gracefully into the afternoon air.

"Anybody else?" asked Roy.

The Devils were silent. The new Devil leader turned to his tattered force. "Okay, you heard the man, let's get them slaves and get the hell out of here."

Six or seven Radleps held the Mean Brother at bay, each with their rifle leveled at his broad chest. The giant stood tense, trying to figure how many of these hideous creatures he could kill before they took him out. Even his great strength gave him no hope. He could see that if he moved an inch he would be dead. Despite his size and his single-minded determination to do damage to his enemies, the Mean Brother was not a stupid man. He knew that it would be better to let them think they had him now and hope for a chance to strike at his captors at a later date.

Roy wandered over and examined his captive closely.

"Big fucker, ain't you?" he said through his cracked and scarred lips.

"You want him greased, boss?" asked one of the 'leps. The Radleps knew well that many of their brother freaks had died at the huge hands of the Mean Brothers. Killing one, shooting one down like an animal, would be a very sweet revenge for them.

"Nawwww," screeched Roy. "Let's take him along. Old man Farkas might be able to use him. If not, there's always some kinda fun we can have with a big fuck like that."

"I say kill the freak now," said one of the leps.

"Since when does anyone do what you say, sport?" demanded Roy.

"Sorry, boss."

"Get some chain. And fix the ugly good and tight. If he escapes it's your ass."

"Yes, boss."

Chaining a Mean Brother is no easy task. But the Brother was almost docile as a double, then a triple length of heavy chain was wound round his wrists and then looped around his neck. The 'leps loaded him into the back of one of the trucks and attached the chain to a heavy metal strut that supported the steel sides of the truck cab. Four 'leps climbed into the back with him keeping their rifles trained on his broad chest.

The Mean Brother had been chained once before in his life and he didn't like it. It was all he could do to keep his volcanic temper in check as he was bound and shackled. As he lay on the floor of the truck he gently tested the strength of the chains. He was pretty sure he could pry them apart given the time but he knew that once free the 'leps that surrounded him would cut him down in a matter of seconds. He thought that there might be a chance that they would become distracted or doze or more or less lose interest in him but he doubted it. These were Radleps and they were mad. If they had been Devils or Stormers they might have opened a chink in their armor and the Mean would have exploited it for all it was worth. He would have killed them all.

He had one hope remaining. Bonner was out there and so was his brother. If they knew he was alive they would come for him. The Mean Brother knew that eventually that they would come for him because he knew that his friends would want to know if he lived or died. If his body wasn't at the battlefield then the Mean Brother knew it was only a matter of time before they showed up. Then his enemies would pay. With that comforting thought in his head, the Mean Brother fell asleep.

The remaining slaves were loaded into the other truck, the Devils and the Radleps mounted their motorcycles and within a few minutes the column was moving again.

A few miles behind them Bonner and the Lash followed, determined to track the column to its destination. Unknown to the 'leps they had been observed by the two Lashmen scouts all through the afternoon and, when they had seen enough they returned to their column to report.

"There are a fuck of a lot of 'em," said one.

"We knew that," said Floyd irritably.

"Too many to attack again," said Bonner.

"Well," said Floyd, "once they get to Farkas' there are only going to be more of them."

"Any sign of the other Mean Brother," asked Bonner.

"Yep," said one of the scouts, "they got him. They got him trussed up good. He don't move except that he's got a dozen 'leps around him. If the big boy is thinking of making a break he's dead meat." The scout punctuated his statement with a wide slash of spit expertly ejected onto the dusty ground.

"Your brother is alive," Bonner said to the remaining Mean Brother, "and we're gonna get him back."

"I'd like to know how," said Rufus.

"We're gonna attack the slave farm," said Bonner simply.

"Swell," said Rufus

"They won't be expecting it," said Floyd, "like the man said."

"I'll believe it when I see it."

The Lashmen moved out and kept their distance well back from the 'lep and Devil column. A relay of scouts kept the enemy in sight, returning every so often to the slower moving column to report on progress. When the Devil column stopped for the night, so did Bonner's men. He passed an order: "No fires."

It was a wise move. He knew that Radleps couldn't help but look for trouble—and they weren't heavy sleepers. Some men swore that they didn't sleep at all. The pain of their horrible, burnt bodies kept them awake night after night until they turned in their agony and sleeplessness into that most feared brand of Radlep: the Psycho 'lep.

The Psychos would wander around their campsites at night searching for spies and marauders that might be lying back just over the horizon. Let a Psycho know you were around and there was no telling how much trouble you would be buying yourself.

The night was passed in miserable silence. No hot food, no fire to keep the exhausted Lashmen warm. Each man lay huddled with his memories of the bloody day, the screams of their brothers lost to Devil and 'lep fire and their fear for the future. The only thing that kept them warm was their hate, their iron-willed determination to meet their enemies again. And triumph.

Rufus, however, wasn't thinking any of this. He was thinking of his own brand of warmth. Emily was asleep on the far side of the camp.

"All curled up," he whispered to himself. "All curled up in a little ball . . ." He licked his lips and thought of Emily's clear blue eyes and red lips. "And them long, long legs . . ." None of the Lashmen would admit it but they always went for tall women.

"She's so warm and I'm so cold," he hissed to himself. He rolled over on his back and looked at the starry sky. "So what the fuck am I doing here?" he asked himself.

Stealthily he pushed aside his dirty blanket and wandered away from the camp. He knew there were a couple of sentries posted around. He wanted to find one.

Looming up out of the darkness came a tiny figure. Rufus could hear the clip as a round was put into a chamber.

"Who the fuck is that?" demanded a voice.

"Rufus. Who's that?"

"Henry."

"Hey, Hank," said Rufus affably, "your watch is up."

"You're early."

"So?"

"First fuckin' time in history you been early for watch."

"Couldn't sleep. Count your blessings."

"Believe me, I am."

"Who else is around?"

"Solly."

"Where?"

"How the fuck should I know? It's dark."

"You gotta fine brain there, Henry."

"Fuck you," said Henry by way of good night.

Rufus strolled around in the dark for a few minutes just to see if he could find the other sentry. He couldn't but it didn't worry him much.

"Fuck him," he muttered. Rufus thought of the young girl that he was about to get close to. Right then nothing else mattered. He circled around the camp, sensing rather than seeing the sleeping bodies on his left. He had taken the precaution of memorizing where Emily lay before all the light had been lost. He was pretty sure he could find her. He also remembered where her protectors, Bonner and the remaining Mean Brother, slept. He was going to have to take her very quietly.

Something awoke Emily a split second before Rufus' dirty paw closed over her soft mouth. In the darkness she could see nothing although her eyes opened wide in fear.

"Now you be good," whispered Rufus. "You be a good little girlie."

Emily thrashed and tried to scream. Rufus' strong arm grasped her about the shoulders, pinioning her in a tangle of blankets. He thrust his rough hand down the front of her soft denim shirt and closed it over the warm, silken mound of her small breast.

"Nice, oooh nice," said Rufus hoarsely. He pushed his hand down further, over the tight stomach. He could feel her belly muscles clenching and unclenching as she sobbed behind his hand.

"Now come on, honey," he whispered, "don't be like that, you'll enjoy it . . ." He forced his hand further down, passed the waistband of her homespun trousers. He fumbled with the buttons that ran from the belt buckle to the crotch. He yanked them open, pulling a button off in the process.

With one hand still bruising her lips, Rufus fumbled with the belt of his own pants, all the while leaning between Emily's legs, trying to pry them apart with his weight. He flopped on top of her and she felt, suddenly, the tip of his cock nosing about between her legs. In his haste, though, Rufus' hand slipped slightly and Emily bit down hard on the side of his hand. She clamped her jaws together, piercing the skin and she tasted the man's blood in her mouth. She bit so forcefully that it seemed to Rufus that her strong white teeth had cut through his hand completely.

He screamed: "Motherfucker!" And tore his hand away from her mouth, leaving there a smear of fresh blood. Then Emily screamed. Instantly the camp was awake.

Rufus fell over waving his hand around as if he had burned himself and tripping and falling in his baggy pants that were tangled around his legs.

"You bitch! You bitch!" he yelled.

Then he felt a very strong hand close on his shoulder. Bonner's.

Bonner yanked him into the air, the little guy's feet dancing a few feet off the ground. Out of the blackness came Bonner's fist, smacking him hard on the side of the jaw.

As Bonner's fist hit, the big man let Rufus go. Rufus flew out into the darkness a few feet and landed with a thud.

"You're dead, motherfucker," screamed the midget. He pulled a knife from his belt and came at Bonner hard and fast. The Outrider stood his ground, tensed and ready for Rufus' attack. Someone else would have figured that with two and a half feet in height and a couple of hundred pounds in weight on the little guy Rufus didn't pose much of a threat—but Bonner had seen bigger men brought down by smaller members of the Lash.

Before Rufus hit a small figure stepped between them. He clotheslined Rufus and before the midget hit the ground busted him hard in the side of the head with his fist.

"He's one of mine, Bonner," said Floyd, "I'll take him."

Rufus had scrabbled to his feet again and was circling the small dark blot on the night that was Floyd.

"It's about fuckin' time, man," said Rufus, "we been coming to this, you 'n' me." He rushed at Floyd. The Lash leader grabbed Rufus' knife hand and held the blade clear. With his other hand he smashed his fist into the attacker's stomach, doubling the little guy over. Before Rufus went down though, he butted Floyd hard on the breastbone, throwing him back in a stagger.

"Prick," gasped Floyd.

Rufus was up again and heading towards Floyd with the blade. When Rufus was close enough, Floyd kicked his assailant very neatly in the balls. Rufus shrieked, retched, and went down for good. Floyd stood on the wrist that controlled the knife and kicked his brother short guy right in the head.

"You make a lot of noise, you know that?" But Rufus didn't hear him. He was out.

Floyd walked back to Bonner. "The only reason I didn't kill the fuck is that he's a good gun and we're gonna need him. Sorry about the little pussy. It won't happen again."

"You know what will happen if he tries anything again," came Bonner's voice from the dark.

"You won't have to, tall man. I'll do it."

Chapter Thirteen

Roy, the tall, scarred Radlep commander, felt a little better about his mission now that he had had the chance to slice up some riders. The fact that they had captured one of the Mean Brothers was an excellent sign. It meant that Bonner was riding with the Lashmen, and if Roy the Radlep knew the Outrider, Bonner would be back.

Until his 'lep column had come upon the Devil's getting their asses kicked by Bonner and the midgets Roy had hated this duty. He didn't think that it was the place of Leather's elite Radleps to be plodding across the country providing escort duty and picking up slaves. Leather had men to do that sort of thing, men that Roy plainly thought of as inferiors. There were Stormers and slavers and torturers in Leather's employment who could have done this job, freeing up the 'leps for the real business of the bomb-broken world: finding Leather's enemies and killing them.

But the sudden appearance of Bonner had changed all that. If the job had been left to the Stormers, they would be dead now—so would the Devils. The slaves would be free and Leatherman's wishes would not have been carried out.

Hidden in a large truck that followed the 'lep column was an important piece of cargo, a man. The man was named Jojo, they called him "fat Jojo" behind his back, but next to Leatherman he was the most important man in the Slavestates. He wasn't much of a fighter—in fact, he wasn't a fighter at all. He was Leatherman's chief counselor and the man who carried Leather's orders from the man himself to the subjects in his empire.

Jojo was on the road heading for Farkas' at Leather's command and it was up to Roy and his Radleps to see that he made it okay. Anyone that tried to stop him had to be killed. As soon as the 'lep column had sighted the battle at the drive-in, Jojo's luxuriously appointed truck had pulled over and the 'leps had been sent on ahead to clear the way. Jojo had lolled in the back of the truck with a slave woman or two and six 'leps standing guard while Roy had taken the column forward to help out the Silk Devils who had been sent out to "escort" the 'lep column into the Hotstates.

Up till then Roy's job had been wetnursing Jojo down the road. He hated that. Jojo never—or almost never—went out on the road and he was scared from the moment he left the Cap, Leatherman's headquarters. It was no use telling him that you couldn't get much safer than having a couple of dozen Radleps around to provide protection. As far as Jojo was concerned the road was a plain old dangerous place to be. He almost fainted when Roy told him that Bonner had been the enemy they had driven off.

"Didja kill him?" asked Jojo, his piggy little eyes full of hope and fear.

"Nope," rasped Roy.

"But you fucked up his riders right? I mean, he ain't coming back, right?"

Roy looked at the fat little man with contempt. "He's coming back," he said tersely and then tied the bandanna across his mouth again. His lips were sore and the wind made it seem like he had a little fire burning in the middle of his face.

"I'm warning you, Roy," screamed Jojo, "If Bonner gets within a mile and a half of me there's gonna be a shitstorm that you won't come out of alive."

Roy's ripped-up features tightened. No one threatened a Radlep, particularly a Radlep commander—and especially not a little fat man who didn't know one end of a shooter from another.

The 'lep column moved on, eating up the miles that would bring them to Farkas' slave farm. They couldn't get there fast enough for Roy. The sooner they got there and Jojo and Farkas did their business, the sooner Roy and his men could be back on the road. As soon as they were on the road again, he expected Mr. Bonner to come calling. It never occurred to Roy that Bonner would try anything at the slave farm itself. It was too heavily defended.

Roy was not a man who could read. If he could have he probably would never have done it anyway. Bonner read and once he had come upon a quote: "Those who ignore the mistakes of history are doomed to repeat them." Roy, and just about everybody else, was sure that Bonner would not attack the farm. But they had all too soon forgotten, that once, not long before, Bonner had lead a small force deep into the heart of the Slavestates and struck the Cap itself. No place was better defended than the Cap, yet the Outrider had hit them there and had triumphed.

One of Jojo's bodyguards came buzzing up the line of the column and pulled in next Roy on the lead bike. Jojo's man pushed back his goggles, tearing the disintegrating skin around his eyes.

"The fat fuck wants to know how long."

Roy never took his eyes off the road ahead of him. "Tell him soon."

The rider pulled out, circled the column and headed back to Jojo.

It sure would be a shame, thought Roy, if in the fight on the way back, Jojo happened to take a stray slug someplace nice and painful and, maybe, fatal.

Just before dusk the 'lep column pulled over a rise and saw the slave farm laid out in front of them. Even Roy was impressed.

It seemed as if the whole valley beneath them was filled with neatly cultivated fields, stretching from one side of the valley to the other. They were green and lush, living things lined in neat rows, lovingly cared for. It was a strange sight in the eyes of men used to seeing a dead or dying world. The lead 'leps rubbed their eyes as if it was all a mirage.

A warm breeze blew and carried a sweet smell up from the fields. It was the smell of freshness and growth, of the natural renewal of the earth. It seemed as if one small part of the shattered continent had been spared the awful destruction that had rained down all over the land. But the impression was a false one. Every man in the column, every man who had ever heard of Farkas' place knew that it was not the paradise it looked to be. It was ruled, like the rest of the world, with the law of the whip and the bullet—life meant nothing.

That much was clear when you caught sight of the compound. Set in the middle of the neatly tended fields was an ugly bruise of gray land. The very center of the compound was dominated by the Old House, Farkas' personal palace. It was an ancient dwelling, built who knows when. The front was lined with a row of stately white pillars, fronting a wide verandah and supporting a high, elegant pediment. The house was cast in two wings on either side of the pillars, a hundred yards each of windows that looked out onto willow trees heavy with age and Spanish moss.

On all sides of the house, as if contrasting with the splendor of the master's house, were row upon row of mean, wooden huts, long, decrepit shacks. The slave quarters. The whole huge compound was surrounded by an eleven-foot barbed-wire fence, patrolled by Farkas' men and Farkas' dogs. At each corner stood a guard tower in which a marksman lolled, hoping that one of the slaves in the square below would crack and make a dash for freedom.

The guards played a little game with the dashers—those slaves who suddenly dashed for the wire. When they were good and tangled in the razor-sharp fence they would take turns shooting at the poor wretch. Any one of the men could have killed the creature with one shot, but it was more fun to knick and slash with the bullets—an ear, a kneecap—until the slave screamed for the killing bullet. Sometimes the force of a slug would dislodge the slave from the wire and he would slide down the wire, tearing himself to ribbons. The guards called them bouncers.

Needless to say, no one had escaped. An even if they had, there was no place to go. In front of the compound was the only road into the valley. Anyone traveling on foot along that road would be spotted and destroyed in a matter of hours. The parts of the valley beyond the "front door" and the cultivated fields were encircled by an inhospitable stew of swamps and tar pits each holding its own terrors. The swamps were trackless wastes of water and sand populated by an unpleasant and unforgiving collection of snakes and alligators. The tar pits were hot, slimy acres of bubbling blackness that would swallow a man up and burn his flesh from his bones as it consumed him.

There was no way out of Farkas' slave farm—at least there was no way out to freedom. Although, a lot of slaves considered death freedom and longed for it every day. It wasn't unheard of for a slave to dash for the wire in the faint hope that an "unlucky" shot would hit him clean in the brain and release him from the daily torment of a terrible enslavement.

All this is not to say that slaves didn't leave the farm, they did and in large numbers. The business of Farkas' slave farm was business: Farkas grew crops but he grew something more valuable than cotton, potatoes, and tobacco. He grew people.

There were the birthing sheds at the farm that looked like a battery house for hens. Only chickens weren't there; women, rather, were installed in the narrow beds, and relays of other slaves did their best to keep them pregnant all the time. But Farkas didn't see any point in keeping the women well fed or clothed or warm—it would cut into profits—so by their third pregnancy in three years they died, usually of exhaustion. But that was okay. A percentage of the babies born were female and so by the time they had reached their tenth year or so they were judged ready for the birthing sheds. Farkas liked to explain that the whole process had taken a lot of years to get working right, but he explained with pride that he had had the vision to plan ahead.

"Quick profits," he would say, "are not the goal of the thinking man."

What he didn't know was that Bonner too was a thinking man and his profits were taken in revenge, not money. Vengeance couldn't buy you much in the bazaars in the Cap or Chi-town, but it helped you sleep better at night.

Farkas wasn't the great planner he thought he was. And his own mismanagement was the reason that Almost Normal had ceased to exist. Unexpectedly, Leatherman had put in an order for a large number of slaves, men and women, and they had to be in top condition. Farkas simply didn't have the stock on hand to accommodate the most powerful man on earth, so he sent his men out to find the mythical town where men and women grew strong and free. The order was simple: Find them and bring them back so Farkas could snatch away their freedom and sell them to to Leatherman.

Jojo was there to negotiate the sale—a sale that Farkas was looking forward to.

The Radlep column had been spotted long before it was close to the slave farm so by the time they reached the compound the tall barbed-wire gates had been thrown open and Farkas himself was standing on the cool balcony of his palace awaiting Jojo.

The 'leps roared into the forecourt in front of the mansion in true Radlep style. The air throbbed with the powerful, gut-twirling sound of perfectly tuned machinery. The big bikes stopped short in front of

Farkas and each rider sat astride his powerful steed waiting for the order to dismount. Jojo's truck lumbered in after them and following him were the tattered and battered bikers of the Devil column that had been sent out to destroy the town of Almost Normal and to bring the Slavestate visitors to the slave farm. Farkas, standing on the balcony with his right-hand man, Paulie, at his side took one look at his men and knew they had been in trouble. He didn't like that. It made him look bad.

"Get those Devils out of here," he said to Paulie. "They look like shit. Kill a couple of them. But quiet."

Paulie nodded and stole away.

Farkas continued to look at the 'lep column. He had heard that Leather was in trouble, that he couldn't control his empire. Well, thought Farkas, if there were any more at home like these, Leather could slice up the Hots, the Snows and have enough left over to take on the riders in Chicago. Farkas was impressed.

One of Jojo's slaves placed a set of wooden steps at the rear of his truck and swept back the canvas curtain that sheltered the occupants of the payload. Jojo poked his head out into the early evening light and then waddled down the steps.

Farkas strolled down from his balcony to meet him.

"Farkas," said Farkas extending a hand.

"Yeah, right," said Jojo. He looked around him. "Nice joint."

Farkas, a tall man dressed head to toe in black looked down at the little man and thought: you little fuck, don't patronize me. "We call it home," he said smiling.

Chapter Fourteen

Bonner and the Lash lay well back from the Farkas spread. They couldn't afford to be spotted or heard before they were ready to make their deadly move. To be seen or detected before they were ready to attack meant that they would be surrendering their most valuable weapon surprise. The Lash were fabulous fighters and Bonner was about as good as you could get and still be human, but without the weight of a sudden unexpected strike behind them, a jab as powerful as a steel-tipped lightning bolt into the heart of Farkas' evil empire, they knew they would lose.

There was a little grumbling from the Lashmen as they stashed their bikes on the grassy slopes of the hills that ringed Farkas' land. They wanted to go in then, right now. They weren't hotheads spoiling for a fight like Stormers and Devils—despite their diminutive stature the Lashmen had nothing to prove when it came to their skill with gun or blade—they thought that going in right away was a wise move.

Some of them wanted to follow the 'lep and Devil column right in, going in on their coattails. They reasoned that they would be able to use the sound of the heavy bikes and trucks as cover for their own approach. Besides, if they were going to take the tough guys by surprise, what better time to go zooming in all guns blazing than when Farkas was welcoming his honored guests to his humble home? Hitting the slave farm would be a surprise, but hitting it right then—who the fuck would think it?

Bonner listened carefully to the idea and he found a lot to admire in the gutsy plan. But the little guys had overlooked the fact that all the 'leps would be on display and that there would be a heavy complement of Silk Devils wandering around to impress the 'leps with Farkas' own firepower. Better to wait for the night.

Neither Bonner nor Floyd, nor any of the other Lashmen had laid eyes on the slave farm before and, well in advance of an attack, Bonner wanted to get a close look at what they were headed into. There was no substitute, Bonner had learned long ago, for reconnaissance. If you knew the lay of the land, where your enemy was strongest and where he was weakest, you had gone a long way towards helping yourself down the road to victory. It was ignoring fundamentals like that that had killed so many riders on the road. They thought that if they had a weapon full of slugs and some guts and gas they could sail along and take anybody down just 'cause they were meaner.

The great riders, people like Bonner, Beck, Seth, the old Outriding crew, they lived and breathed the basics of warfare. If you don't get sloppy, you don't get killed. It was that simple.

But Farkas was going to be a tough nut to crack. Bonner wanted to get close, real close, to the set-up and find out everything he could about it before he committed his savage, valiant fighters to the all-out struggle to destroy the horror ranch that filled the peaceful valley before them. That meant going in, snooping around, searching for all the chinks in the mighty armor. Bonner wanted to live with the beast before he killed it.

And that was going to be tough. Bonner smiled to himself when he thought about the day—it seemed like a year before—when he had sworn to take down Farkas all by himself. Even he could get hotheaded sometimes. He looked around him. The Lashmen lay in the shadows of their bikes enjoying the cool calm of the afternoon. To the uninitiated, they would look like a bunch of guys without a care in the world. But Bonner knew that each one of them was thinking of the enemy that lay just over the rise of the hill. They were hardy, crazy little killers and Bonner was glad, very glad, to have them on his side.

Floyd thrashed through the long grass, making his

way towards the Outrider. The little man could hardly be seen as he wended his way through the weeds, the tip of his gun barrel alone showing, glistening slightly in the sunlight. He paused next to Bonner.

"Well," he said, sniffing the fresh air, "Farkas sure found a nice little spot on this old Continent to spread his shit around."

Bonner looked around him. The hills were green, the valleys between them spoke of pasture and plenty. It was pretty country now, it must have been prettier before the bomb gave men like Farkas the power to rule over it.

"Yeah," said Bonner, "Good land . . ."

"Ya gotta say one thing for the old Leatherman, at least he keeps to himself, sorta, up in that ole pile of shit in the Cap. Ya know—" Floyd yanked a piece of grass out of the ground, sucked it, then jammed it into the space between his two big yellow front teeth. "—ya know, I traveled all over the Slavestates and I never seen a part of it that ain't shit. Dirty old rubbletowns, black earth, slimebag rivers. Dead, all of it dead. You know what I mean?"

Bonner nodded. There were parts of the Slavestates that weren't bad, up north mostly, along the sea, but for the most part, Floyd spoke the truth. Mostly the Slavestates were a pit filled with memories of a dead past and a violent present, sucked dry and terrorized by a bad and greedy man that Bonner swore to kill.

"So Leather," continued Floyd philosophically, "he's crap keeping company with crap, you know? Shit living on garbage, you see what I mean?"

"Yeah," said Bonner, wondering just what Floyd was getting to.

"Now this guy Farkas, the way I see it, he's just set himself down here in this pretty place and he's doing nothing but getting himself rich and making the place ugly. And you know what?"

"What," said Bonner, as if he was expecting a punch line.

"Well, I'll tell you. Not only does it piss me off, it offends me."

Bonner smiled. "Me too."

"So what we gonna do about it?"

"Well," said Bonner, "first I want to go down there and take a closer look."

"Good idea. The more we know about them the better we can flatten them."

"Something like that."

"When you goin'?"

"Tonight."

"Alone."

"Yep."

"You're crazy. And you ain't goin' alone. You're going to need some firepower for sure if you get in a jam."

Bonner had thought of that. His decision to scout the slave farm alone was not born of some lone-gun heroics. Ideally, three men would have made the best-sized force to bring down the valley to the Farkas spread. But right now there were problems . . .

"You know you could use some help," said Floyd. "Take a couple of us."

"You're right," said Bonner, "but look, I'm going to try and get inside the wire."

"Yeah. So?"

"Well, suppose I get inside the wire and I get spotted?"

"Then you'll get your ass shot off."

"That wasn't the answer I was looking for."

Floyd looked puzzled. "There's another answer."

"Yes," said Bonner, "there is. It'll be dark. There's a chance they'll think I'm one of their guys. We can't afford to get shot at. We don't want to wake the whole place up."

"I still don't get it."

"Floyd, how is it going to look if I'm down there with a couple of midgets?"

"Yeah? And what if they see you and they start shooting? Then you only got one chance, to blast your way out of there. Then you gonna need a couple of extra guns along."

"Floyd, if they start shooting then we're all screwed because then they aren't going to lay down long enough for us to take them."

Floyd exhaled deeply, as if he was angry but trying to hold it in, not to show it. "Then stay the fuck out, okay? Don't go. When it's dark we'll sneak down to the wire and start killing the fucks."

"If we get an idea of what things are like down there we can hit them twice as hard."

The midget leader rested his hands on his hips. "Maybe, but I say you gotta take a couple of guns along. Shit, man, I wanna go. It'll be fun. Me and a couple of other guys and you. If they see us maybe they'll think it's you and a couple of kids . . ."

"Kids," said Bonner.

"Hey," said Floyd, "there's an idea. Them kids are tall enough. They could pass. Give 'em some shooters and take them."

"Don't be a jerk, Floyd," said Bonner. The kids were inexperienced and he had no right to endanger them. If there was trouble they would end up just getting in the way.

"Then take your monster with you."

"Maybe." The Mean Brother was a master of the silent kill, that was for sure. But he sure was easy to see.

"Won't do you no harm."

"He sorta stands out in a crowd, though," said Bonner.

"That's for fuckin sure. Listen, just don't go alone, okay?"

He won't, thought Bobby. He was lying on his stomach a few feet from where the fighters stood, concealed by the tall weeds.

Chapter Fifteen

The night was Bonner's friend. While other men feared the darkness, Bonner welcomed it. He knew that a night fighter was the most deadly, dangerous type of warrior there was, one who could do untold damage to his enemies, silently and unseen. But you had to befriend the darkness. You had to learn how to use it, to wear it, donning it as you might a worn, comfortable leather jacket. You couldn't resist the blackness, you had to adopt an easy familiarity with its all-encompassing grip on your senses and vision. There was no big picture: the few feet ahead that you could see had to become your world.

Tiny sounds, an inch or two of visibility had to be seized and used to your advantage. If you knew how to do it, to work in the night rather than against it, you became deadly. From the darkness a man could attack, quiet and unseen, using a blade as deadly and silent as the night itself. The men that cowered in fear of the night, praying for daybreak, they were the men condemned to die in it.

Bonner had decided against taking the Mean Brother with him. Sure, he was silent and dangerous, but he was just too big, not stealthy enough to wade through the black without making a sound. The Mean Brother had looked very disappointed when Bonner told him of his decision, but Bonner had spoken and that was good enough for the Mean.

Bonner made his way down the valley sides quietly, although he didn't know the ground. He proceeded slowly, unsure whether or not there might be patrols in the foothills and fields that surrounded the slave farm. He doubted it, he paused every few yards to listen for voices and footsteps and heard nothing. He imagined that Farkas and his lieutenants thought themselves too well protected to bother with something as cautious as patrols.

By the time Bonner reached the valley floor the moon was high and the fields and farm were bathed in a silvery light. From within the compound came some sounds: a burst of song, a shout of laughter. Bonner figured that Farkas' men spent most of their evenings drinking their master's booze and carousing. There wasn't much else to do.

Bonner was making fairly easy going of it through the regular rows of trees in an orchard. Once he got close to the wire he was going to have to take a long, hard look at the compound before deciding where to enter it. Thrust into the belt of his pants was a set of heavy wire cutters. He hoped he would be able to find a remote part of the wire and let himself in without doing too much damage to the fence.

A sound, a footfall, reached his ears. He froze. There was someone near. Bonner was sure he could hear the man breathing. Carefully, he mentally divided the blackness around him into quadrants and checked each black box, peering into the gloom with his eyes, listening hard until he thought he could hear the circulation of his own blood.

On either side of him were trees. A man could be concealed behind any one of them. Bonner took another step then stopped. He sensed the bulk of a man flying out of the darkness before he saw him. Bonner half turned and saw, above him, a man, a big man barreling towards him in a flying tackle. One gloved hand held a knife. Bonner knew, in the second before impact who the foe was: a Psychlop, another night fighter.

The hard body of the man scythed into Bonner and he fell, he hand dropping to his side to pull his one of his own blades from his belt. Bonner's other hand shot up and grabbed the raw, red wrist of the 'lep's knife hand.

Bonner caught the horrible, rotting stench of the 'lep. It seemed to flood his nostrils and make him gag. It clung to the inside of his throat like glue.

The man hissed through broken teeth, his hideous

scarred face almost on Bonner's own: ". . . kill you . . ."

The 'lep was strong. Bonner could feel the freak-man's hate-powered muscles working like hydraulics forcing his knife-wielding hand down towards Bonner's throat. The terrible stench the man gave off triggered a flow of bitter bile from Bonner's gut. He spat. The warm juice slashed across the 'lep's face and he pulled back for a second, long enough for Bonner's knife hand to break the hold which the freak held it. He buried the blade deep in the 'lep's back.

The sudden pain and unexpected humiliation of the drawing of first blood, caused the 'lep to pull away, his body twisting, like a fish suddenly dropped in the bottom of a boat. The sudden wrench made Bonner let go of the handle of his blade. Anger and pain drove the wide slash of the 'lep's blade. If he had thought about it, he would have killed Bonner, but he struck without considering his blow. The tip slipped across the thin skin of his forehead, carving a fine four-inch line of blood there. Blood cascaded down into Bonner's eyes, blinding him.

He couldn't fight blind, so he rolled left, hoping that he could avoid the second, more carefully planned fall of the 'lep's knife.

Maddened by the pain of the blade that still lodged in his back, the 'lep twisted his hand around to reach it. But the wicked eight inches of steel was beyond his grasp. He tried to clear his brain long enough to dispatch Bonner. He swung again.

Bonner had cleared his eyes of blood long enough to catch the knife hand again. But this is where the Psycholep had him. The scarred man was crazy with hate and pain—and he knew that the waggling blade in his back would probably kill him. So he must kill this man before him. To die without having destroyed the man that killed you was the ultimate 'lep disgrace.

Bonner on the other hand was not fatally injured. But he was blinded and weakened. He summoned every ounce of energy in his body, the last atom of strength he possessed to keep the 'lep knife hand from delivering the fatal blow. He couldn't see. His own warm blood trickled into his eyes and on down his face, pooling on his chest.

Then, when he least expected it, he heard a sound that reminded him of the smack of an axe against a stout tree. The arm of the 'lep went limp. Bonner dashed one hand into his blood-clogged eyes and rubbed enough away to look up and see that the 'lep had been attacked from behind. A huge machete blade was buried two inches deep in his torn skull, the point of the blade neatly halving his forehead—it looked as if the freak warrior had suddenly and unexpectedly grown a rusty metal horn. The 'lep's bloodshot eyes swiveled in his head, as if trying to look up at the shaft of metal that slashed through his brain. As he toppled off Bonner the man's long thin arm swished out behind him, as if he was trying, hoping, to catch his unseen attacker with the tip of his blade.

But the blow was weak, and Bobby just brushed the man aside. The 'lep fell like a chopped down tree.

Bobby dropped to his knees next to Bonner and tried to wipe away the blood that robbed the Outrider of his sight. Bonner still did not know who his saviour was.

"Who the hell is that?" he gasped.

"It's me, Bobby."

Bonner felt as if he had been struck by lightning. He sat up. "What the hell are you doing here."

"I . . . I followed you . . ."

Bonner was about to get angry, then he changed his mind.

"Damn good thing, too," he said. As he spoke he slipped the second of his knives out of the holster and roughly chopped the sleeve of his shirt off. With the rag he mopped up the blood on his face and forehead and then tied it around his head so it could catch the blood that still seeped from the wound.

Then he looked at Bobby. The kid had taken his first kill. A Psycholep—a creature that had probably killed more men, women, and children than Bobby had seen days in his young life. The kid showed no emotion. Bonner would have expected that he would be trembling or upset or even in tears—Bonner had seen riders real shook up after a close-quarters fight with a less dangerous foe than a Psycholep. But the kid showed nothing, not a hint of emotion. Bonner wondered if this was because the kid didn't know, or he just didn't care.

"You know what that was," Bonner said, gesturing towards the dead man.

"Some 'lep," said the kid. "You want me to pull out your knife?"

"Yeah," said Bonner. "And does Floyd know you stole his machete?"

"He probably does by now," said Bobby with a hint of a smile.

"Then we better get it out of the 'lep's head and back to him."

"You gonna look around more tonight?"

Bonner thought about the throbbing pain in his forehead. He had a headache that felt like someone was pounding on his temples with a sledgehammer. "Yeah," he said, "we better do some."

"We?" said Bobby hopefully.

"Sure." Bonner smiled. "If we run into more Psycholeps you'd be a good man to have around.

It seemed to Bonner that the kid lit up the darkness with his beaming face. Getting the machete out of the 'lep's head was no easy matter. It was also messy. It was only then that Bonner saw Bobby cringe a little.

"Welcome to the real world, kid," thought Bonner.

═══════════════════════Chapter Sixteen

Bonner and Bobby did their reconnaissance and then beat it back to the camp where the Lashmen lay concealed. By the time they got back to their hiding place the beginnings of the new day were peeking over the horizon. The air was still and the lush grass was wet with dew. In the half light of dawn Bonner looked back at the slave ranch. Already, the spread was beginning to echo with the shouts of the slave overseers and a cookhouse chimney was shooting some gray smoke into the clear sky.

Some of the slaves would be assembled and marched off to the fields. Others would be gathered for manual labor around the grounds of the camp. Bonner figured there was even a contingent that took care of Farkas in the big house, household servants. Bonner hoped that if he and the Lashmen failed one day the slaves that Farkas had let in the front door would slice the big man's throat. Someone had to do it eventually.

Bonner heard a sharp crack slice through the morning air. Even from where he stood, quite a ways from the house, he could tell what the sound was—the savage tongue of a lash making contact with skin. Obviously, some slave had not moved fast enough for his master's liking. Bonner had seen what those whips could do. A single lick could lay a man's back open to the bone. Bonner wondered how many of the slaves down there were hoping as they awoke that this would be their last day on earth. A chance remark, a sneer, a joke might push one of their keepers to a fury that would reward the slave with a single clean bullet. He would die with a smile on his face.

Just before he disappeared over the rise, Bonner looked at the house. It was still and silent. The emperor did not rise with his empire. Farkas would get up late, bathe, eat, and generally be attended to by his servants, each day an endless train of pleasures. Those, Bonner swore, were about to come to an end.

Floyd and the rest of the Lashmen were awake. It would be another day without fire, therefore another uncomfortable day without hot food. The attack would have to come soon. Apart from the discomfort, the band of warriors couldn't expect to lie hidden for much longer with the enemy just over the hill. Eventually, they would be discovered.

But right then Floyd didn't give a damn about the attack. When Bonner and Bobby returned he jumped up and one look at his face told Bonner the little guy was mad.

"Where the fuck have you been? And where the fuck do you get off taking my slicer?"

"There was a little trouble," said Bonner quietly, as if afraid his voice would carry.

"Kid, did you take my sword?"

"Yes," said Bobby, "I did."

"You little brat. Dint'ja ever learn not to take shit that didn't belong to you?"

"Yes sir," said Bobby.

"Leave him alone, Floyd," said Bonner. "It was a good thing he came along with that big chopper of yours when he did."

"How do you mean?"

"Bobby cut himself a Psycholep with that thing."

"That little runt?" Bobby stood fully a head taller than the midget leader.

"Yep."

Floyd turned to Bobby. "That true?"

"Yes sir, it is."

"Hell," said Floyd, "I ain't never got me a Psycholep. Not close to, anyhow."

"It was a close thing," said Bonner, "if he hadn't come along I'd be a casualty now."

"Looks like you caught some trouble," said Floyd eyeing Bonner's bandana.

"Would have been worse without Bobby."

Floyd reached out to take the machete away from Bobby. Then he pulled his hand back. "Nawwww. You keep it. If you can use it well enough for taking down a Psycholep you better hang onto it. . . . Just don't take stuff that ain't yours in future, got it."

"Yes, sir."

"And cut out that 'sir' crap. Call me Floyd."

"Okay . . . Floyd."

"Little shit . . ." Floyd's face split in a broken-toothed grin. "Save Bonner's ass, huh? I guess you gonna be as tough a bring down as Bonner some day kid. Hey Bonner, how does it feel to have your skin saved by a kid?"

"Just fine," said Bonner.

"So cut the crap," said Rufus wandering up, "whad'ja find out?"

"Well," said Bonner, it looks like Mr. Farkas is going to throw himself a little party. . . ."

"Party party party. All these Devils ever seem to do is party," said Floyd recalling the sudden firefight at the drive-in.

"I guess it's to entertain their guests."

"Who's with them 'leps?" demanded Rufus.

"Hard to say," said Bonner, "but I'd guess it was someone big."

"Don't spose it's the Leatherman?"

"No, it's not him." There was the faintest whisper of disappointment in the Outrider's voice. "Maybe Jojo."

"That fat fuck. Maybe we can get him and ransom him back to Leather. You know he's Leather's brains . . ."

"Yeah," said Bonner, "maybe . . ." He knew that if he got within a hundred yards of the chancellor of the Slavestates Jojo would very suddenly become a corpse.

"So when do we go in?"

"Tonight," said Bonner.

"About fucking time," observed Rufus.

Farkas lay curled up like a huge worm on his big white draped bed. His mouth was open and he was drooling on the pillow. The small women next to him hiked herself up on an elbow and looked at him. As she did so, a luxuriant curtain of red hair unfurled itself from the bun at the back of her neck and cascaded down about her shoulders. She looked at the man next to her with disgust. She was not a pretty woman, but she wasn't ugly either. Sneery annoyance was the usual cast of her features and it did nothing for her looks.

Farkas honked, then farted. Then scratched his ass with a sound like sandpaper rubbing on rough board.

The woman looked at the ceiling then down at the sleeping brute next to her. She was annoyed and she tried to control it for a second, but decided against it.

"Farkas!" she barked.

Farkas grunted and his bloodshot eyes opened. "Wha'?"

"Wake up, you sonofabitch."

Farkas groaned. It was another day. Another day with the cow, the bitch, the cross he had to bear . . .

"I said wake up!"

"I'm awake, dear."

"Good. Look at me."

Farkas rolled his considerable bulk over to look at the woman.

"You look like shit," she spat.

Farkas nodded. He felt like shit. He had drunk too much the night before and he felt it. He exhaled heavily.

"And your breath!"

"Sorry, dear," said Farkas, averting his mouth.

The little woman's face twisted into a look a barely controlled fury. "You know, you are one fat dumb sonofabitch."

Dimly, memories of what went on the night before came back to him.

"Are you listening to me?"

"Yes, dear." One day, thought Farkas, one day . . . One day he was going to give an order to a couple of his men and this little bitch was going to be carted off and slaughtered. But it wasn't going to be quick. She was going to go out in slow agony. First the tits, then the face . . . Farkas dreamily conjured up the image.

"Do you have any idea how much money you lost last night?"

"Ohhhh, God," said Farkas rolling over. He had been gambling with that little asshole from the Cap.

Dice. "Just one more roll," Farkas had said drunkenly over and over. Farkas couldn't quite remember, but it seemed to him that Jojo hadn't gotten drunk at all. There was going to be trouble about that. Farkas liked to see that his rare guests got good and drunk. He also couldn't quite remember just how much money he had lost. He had no doubt that the bitch next to him was about to let him know to the last penny. One day . . .

"Six thousand slates!" she screeched. "Six thousand! Just one more roll, you kept on saying like a moron. And you were disgustingly drunk!" She pronounced it in four carefully enunciated syllables: dis-gust-ing-ly.

"I'm sorry, honeybun."

"Don't honeybun me," she snapped. "Luckily, you didn't pay him. You said you'd do it this morning."

"Thank goodness," said Farkas. He'd kill the little fucker before he'd pay him six thousand gold ones. He would have to really gouge him on the prices for the slaves also. He snuggled down in the bed and the little woman, figuring that he had had enough, massaged his big shoulders with her strong fingers.

"Ahhhhhhh," said Farkas, feeling the throbbing headache in his forehead begin to disintegrate.

"What would you do without me?" said the woman.

"Dunno," said Farkas. She was working on his neck now and relief was flooding through him.

"You big lug . . ." she said affectionately. She figured that one of two things was about to happen. Either he would fall asleep again or her fingers were working him up in a different direction. If that happened, he would flop over on top of her and, with very little finesse, have quick and sweaty sex with her. She sighed. It was the price you paid for living with a rich man.

As she feared, Farkas' monstrous libido was awakened and he lay on her and for a few minutes he ground her into the fluffy mattress. He came with a number of shouts and sighs and bellows and flopped off her. Thank God, she thought, that's over.

Farkas lay with a happy smile on his face. He knew he would never have her taken away. Strange to say, but big, nasty, brutal, bloodthirsty, savage Farkas loved this little woman.

"I gotta get up," she said.

"Sweety-kins," said Farkas, "stay in beddy with your little Farkas-warkus."

"Make me puke," thought the woman. "Are you crazy," she said aloud, "I've got a million things to do. We are having a party tonight for our honored guest."

"That little prick."

"That little prick is going to buy a hundred thousand slates worth of slaves. We haven't had an order like that in a long time. . . ."

"A hundred and six thousand," said Farkas sourly, thinking of his humiliation the night before.

"What are you going to do with him today?" demanded the woman.

"Show him around. Take him into the sheds. Let him take a look at the stock, you know . . ."

"You stay away from those slave women," she spat. "I find you plowing one of them, and I'll cut your balls off." She was dressing, piling her hair up on top of her head. Her red tresses were a mass of curls and coils. To keep them in place she reached for a glittering selection of small throwing knives that lay arrayed on the night table in front of her. She thrust the little steel hornets into her hair savagely. Farkas watched her. She was no slouch with those knives, Farkas thought, she was a little killer.

He swept back the bed clothes displaying his hairy naked body. "Come on, pussy-willow," said Farkas, "come back to bed with your lovin' man . . ."

Oh, cut me a break, thought the woman, who went by the name of Mrs. Farkas.

=========================**Chapter Seventeen**

Jojo was eating. It was not a pretty sight. He was sitting at a table that had been set up on the wide and shady porch of the old mansion that Farkas called home. The table was spread with a white cloth—rather, it had been white at the beginning of the meal, now it was slopped over with stains. Jojo was, to put it mildly, a messy eater. A slave stood in front of the table ladling more food onto the plate as Jojo called for it. Two Radleps stood behind their master looking around suspiciously, as if they expected Bonner to pop out from behind a bush and start blasting.

The 'leps had reason to be suspicious. A fellow 'lep was missing. The Radleps took it very badly when one of their number disappeared. If he turned up dead, some blood was going to be shed.

At that moment, though, Jojo wasn't worried about

a thing besides filling his big gut. Farkas was an asshole, he thought, but his food was fantastic. The plate in front of him was as big as a hug cap on an old Caddy and it was piled high with a steak the size of a boulder. There was a side of mashed potatoes that stood a full six inches high on the plate, a pound of bacon, and a dozen fried eggs slithering around, wherever there was room. . . .

Jojo was bent double over the food, glowering out from under his eyebrows as if he were ready to kill the man that tried to take his snack from him. His left arm was crooked around the plate, holding it, his right hand was a blur as it shoveled the food into his wide mouth as fast as he could. As his big yellow teeth chopped up the food, some of it tried to escape and stained his lips; bits of mashed potatoes lodged in the scraggly beard that flapped listlessly around his chin like a hairy bib. The slave who served him had seen some ugly sights in his time but watching Jojo eat was about as bad as they came. It turned his hardened stomach. Between Jojo and the two freaks behind his chair, the whole tableau was pretty disgusting.

Farkas came on the scene and eyed his guest from a few feet away. The big slave keeper's reaction to Jojo was much the same as the slaves. Disgusting, thought Farkas.

Jojo didn't think much of Farkas either. He sat back from the plate, belched a burp as loud as a pistol shot, and rubbed his stomach.

"Morning, Jojo," said Farkas.

"You owe me," said Jojo pleasantly.

"I do, huh," said Farkas, "how much?"

"A small matter of a few thousand slates," said Jojo.

"Big fuckin' deal," said Farkas, "don't bother me with these chickenshit numbers. There's real business to be done."

"Well, if it ain't much to a big man like you," said Jojo. He paused to work another belch out of the bushel-basket belly he carried around with him. It came, loud and sulphurous and he finished his sentence. ". . . then maybe you wouldn't mind settling up now."

"Yeah, yeah," said Farkas, as if he couldn't be bothered. Actually he was thinking that if Mrs. Frakas ever found out that he paid Jojo his gambling debt his life would be hell for the next six months. "So how long you gonna be here?"

"Leaving as soon as I fuckin' can," said Jojo.

"We'll settle up when we work out who owes what. I have a feeling you're gonna end up owing me more than I owe you."

"What the fuck does that mean?"

"It means you came to deal, right? So you're gonna buy slaves, right? So who the fuck do you think you're gonna pay for them. Me, right?"

"Don't talk to me like that man," said Jojo quietly, "you know who you're dealing with, right? I'm fuckin' Leatherman's right-hand man. Got it?"

"Yeah," said Farkas, "you're the little fuck that jerks him off right?"

By way of reply, Jojo reached under the big flap of flesh that hung at his waist and grabbed a couple of pounds of pistol that he kept hidden under his gut. He leveled it at Farkas.

"Maybe I'll just blow your head off and take whatever I need. How would that sound."

Farkas laughed. It wasn't the first time he had looked down the barrel of a gun. "Tough man, tough man," he laughed.

Jojo stared at him. He wasn't used to being insulted and he wasn't used to being laughed at, and yet both things had happened inside of ten minutes. And the day had just started.

" 'leps are good," Farkas continued, "hell, I'd be the first to say that. But shit, Jojo, use your head. You only got fifty men here. I got about a thousand. You'd never make it to the gate. And don't forget. Leatherman ain't the only game on the continent, ya know. Berger would never let you get out of the Hots alive."

"Oh, Berger," snorted Jojo, "You're scaring the piss out of me."

"Put the shooter away, Jojo, and we'll be friends again. I got some things planned for today. You'll have a good time."

By way of compromise Jojo put the gun down on the table in front of him, as if it was there if he decided to use it.

"So like what?" demanded Jojo.

"Thought I'd show you around the operation. Let you take a look at the slaves. Make some choices . . . See what you might want. You know, stuff like that . . ."

"What's so special about that? That's what I come here to do."

"Okay, okay," said Farkas. "I *was* keeping it as a surprise . . ."

"What ferchrissakes!"

"We were gonna put on a little show tonight."

"What kind of show?"

"You'll see . . ."

The tour began after Jojo had put away another six or seven pounds of food. Only once he was properly fortified could he attend to the business of the day.

When the plate was licked clean he hoisted himself to his feet and followed Farkas down the graceful steps of the old mansion to the courtyard of the plantation. Farkas noted that Jojo's breathing was labored, as if his heart and lungs objected to carrying around so much blubber.

"The fat fuck is going to eat himself to death," Farkas thought.

"Not so goddam fast," said Jojo.

If anyone had any doubts that Farkas was absolute ruler over his domain, the tour around his property dispelled them. Wherever he went on his property, slaves dropped to their knees as he passed, averting their fear-filled eyes as if he was some sort of god temporarily walking on earth. Jojo had to admit to himself that he was impressed. Not even Leatherman got this kind of respect, and the Leatherman ruled an area measured in hundreds of square miles, not a few lousy acres like Farkas.

"So what do we see first?"

"Thought you might want to take a look at the birthing sheds."

"What the fuck are those."

"What the hell do you think they are," thought Farkas. "Where do you think babies come from?"

The Silk Devil escorting them pushed open the door of one of the sheds that surrounded the main house. Farkas stepped in, with Jojo and his two 'leps following.

The shed was dimly lit and absolutely silent. It took Jojo's eyes a few seconds to adapt to the light, but once his eyes cleared and adjusted, he saw exactly why Farkas called them the "birthing sheds."

The room was filled with beds, three-tiered and caged with chicken wire. Stretched out on each bed, reclining naked on a series of thin mattresses were hollowed eyed women, each in the advanced stages of pregnancy. They stared at Farcas blankly.

"The latest crop," said Farkas proudly, as if he was showing off a new litter of puppies.

"Jeez," said Jojo as he surveyed the room. There must have been two hundred women in the room. "Who porks all these broads?" He asked elegantly.

"The studs," said Farkas, "we call 'em the bulls."

"Haw," said Jojo, "nice work if you can get it."

"You think," said Farkas, shooting his guest a sideways glance. "How would you like to do it seven times a day . . ."

"Haw haw," said Jojo, "I wouldn't kick . . ."

"Day in, day out. Every day of the year. It sounds better than it is."

Farkas walked down the row of beds. He stopped in front of a woman who looked to be about sixty. "My best breeder," said Farkas affectionately.

"Her!" said Farkas. "She looks about ninety-five. I'd say her days are about over."

"How many pups you had, dear?" asked Farkas.

"Twenty-two," croaked the woman.

"And tell the man how old you are?"

"I think thirty," said the woman.

"A little more," sid Farkas, "thirty-three."

"Thirty-three!" said Jojo, doing some quick arithmetic. "You mean you started her when she was eleven?"

"S'right. She's been pregnant ever since."

"Jeez," said Jojo, genuinely impressed.

"They usually cave in after about seven or eight, but some of 'em just keep on producing. The human body is an amazing thing, you know?"

"She don't look so amazing," said Jojo, running his eyes over the woman's swollen belly and emaciated flanks.

"Well, it takes a lot out of them. This one, I doubt she can walk anymore. If she could I might consider retiring her but, you know it ain't worth it . . ." He spoke as if the woman wasn't there. "Her time will come. A lot of them croak during delivery. I got a couple women who deliver the pups, but they don't really know what the hell they're doing. They croak too many cows—we call 'em cows—and they get put in the sheds themselves. It's the best I can do to make sure they do their best."

"Got any that are, you know, good looking?" asked Jojo.

"We got special sheds for the real foxes. Most people who want slaves, they want strong ones. They don't care what they look like, ya' know? The foxes, I mean they can look good, but that don't mean they're gonna have good-looking pups. The ones that turn out good, they are real expensive. Real expensive."

"You unnerstan' that I come looking for full growns," said Jojo. "I don't want to take no kids back to Leather. I want big strong men and women. The best."

"Business later," said Farkas airily. "But just to put your mind at rest, I'll tell you I got some special stock for you."

"When can I see 'em?"

"In a minute. Don't you want to see the bulls?"

"Oh, yeah," snorted Jojo. "Those lucky fucks."

Back in the sunlight, they met a brawny-looking Skag Devil crossing the parade ground.

"Grubby," barked Farkas. The man stopped dead in his tracks, frozen by the sound of Farkas' voice.

"Yes boss?"

"You headed for the bull pen?"

"Yessir, time for the third shift of the day."

"We'll tag along and take a look if you don't mind, that is."

"No problem at all, sir, no problem at all."

Farkas and his guest fell in behind Grubby and followed him to yet another shed that stood nearby. Jojo noticed that the overseer carried neither gun nor whip.

"These guys never get uppity? These bulls?"

Grubby laughed. "No sir, they don't."

They reached the door of a shed and Grubby kicked it open. As he entered a chorus of groans went up from the occupants.

Jojo couldn't believe his eyes. The bulls looked to be in worse shape than the cows. They were thin and washed out looking. Exhausted, clapped out.

"Ker-rist," he said, "these guys look terrible."

"And they're half your age," said Farkas with a chuckle. "Sometimes we use bull duty as a punishment . . . I tell you, fuckin' takes it out of you."

Grubby took a deep breath and started bellowing out numbers. Each bull had a number and the overseers took care to keep track of whose turn it was to climb into the saddle again.

"No," murmured one bull, a balding, broken-toothed man, as thin as a corpse. "Please, not again."

Farkas laughed. "See, Jojo, tole you it wasn't no

picnic. When you fuck a couple of thousand times a year, it just ain't fun no more.''

"Maybe you're right."

"You wanna see them in action. We could go see the fucking sheds now."

"How 'bout we eat instead?" said Jojo.

=============================Chapter Eighteen

Lunch was set up on the same table that Jojo had breakfasted at. When Farkas and Jojo returned to the house—Jojo still panting at the slight exertion of keeping up with his rather slow-moving host—they found Mrs. Farkas seated at the head of the table looking at the two men as if they were children who had come late when called.

"Hi dear," said Farkas.

"Hello, darling," said Mrs. Farkas.

"Just been showing Mr. Jojo here around."

"Very nice," said Mrs. Farkas in a "big fucking deal" tone of voice.

"Very impressive," said Jojo. It was plain to him that Mrs. Farkas was the power to be reckoned with around the slave farm. Her position to her husband was not unlike his own relation to Leatherman. Leather, like Farkas, had to appear to make the decisions, he had to give the orders, take the praise, be looked upon with fear and trembling, while it was the brainy, if less impressive looking types like Jojo and Mrs. Farkas who actually held the empires together. Jojo and Mrs. Farkas eyed one another and each knew that the other was thinking the same thing. They were of the same type, those two, each cut from the same cloth. As long as there were smart, ruthless people like Jojo and Madame Farkas around, the evil dominion of the continent and all the riches it produced would continue. Without people like them, people like Farkas and Leatherman were doomed.

Mr. Farkas had pulled out all the stops for the luncheon she was about to serve to Jojo. The table was spread with a host of pre-bomb delicacies that were almost unheard of in those days. Only the richest men could afford to lay out the rare canned food that the old Americans had taken for granted.

Jojo was not unaware of the honor that was being done him and he appreciated it. The bad temper of the previous night and the strain of the confrontation over breakfast that morning vanished as course followed sumptuous course. Mrs. Farkas was behaving much as Jojo would have had he been entertaining powerful guests that he wanted something from. Flatter them, indulge their greatest appetites and weaknesses. In Jojo's case, food. Of course, they all knew that if you couldn't get what you wanted through polite means, there was always torture and finally, of course, murder. But no one would dare harm Jojo without risking war with Leatherman.

The first course was placed before him and Jojo looked at it with interest. It was a white and red mixture, a sort of stew that he had never seen before. The smell drifted up to his nose and he couldn't wait to try it.

"What's this?" he asked.

Farkas smiled. It was one of his treasures from the pre-bomb larder. He had looked many times at the faded label.

"They're called Spaghetti-O's," said Mrs. Farkas. "I believe that we own the last cans of them on the continent."

Jojo slurped them down. Ambrosia. "Delish," he said, looking around to see if there were any more.

Mrs. Farkas noted his interest and gestured to a slave to bring more. There were only a few cans left and they were more than likely to vanish into the all-consuming maw of Jojo's busy mouth.

After three cans, the second course was announced. Placed in front of Jojo this time was a steaming pile of canned beef stew.

"Ahhhh," said Farkas with the air of a connoiseur, "Dinty Moore . . ."

The third course was the best yet, to Jojo's way of thinking. The Farkas' slaves trotted out the strangest looking foods he had ever seen.

"What the hell is this?" he asked.

"We're not sure," said Farkas. "Except that the

labels say: Chun-King Chow Mein. And that one is something called Chop Suey.''

"Never heard of it," said Jojo.

"They made Chinese swing American," said Mrs. Farkas quoting from the label, as if she knew what it meant.

Side dishes of urine-colored string beans and peas were placed here and there around the table.

"Fresh from the can," said Farkas.

With dessert—"Fluffernutter," explained Mrs. Farkas—came a little light entertainment.

"These were the slaves I thought you might be interested in," said Farkas. Slowly the overseers trotted out the residents of Almost Normal. They differed from the slaves that Jojo was used to seeing. It was like night and day. The men, the women, the children, were tall and strong, looking straight at Jojo and the Farkas without fear. It disconcerted Jojo slightly.

"Home grown?" he asked.

"Of course," lied Madame Farkas easily, hoping that Jojo wouldn't recognize any of the Almost Normals from the slave train he had accompanied in the day before.

"Strong, healthy, and some of 'em are mighty good lookin'," put in Farkas.

"I can see that," said Jojo. They were the finest looking slaves he had seen in a long time. There was something different about this set of people that struck him as totally out of line with the slaves he was used to seeing. How could he have known that it was a simply diet of freedom, hard work for themselves and their families and their friends, years of determining their own future, making their own mistakes, savoring their own triumphs, that had raised these people strong and proud. They were the true descendants of the people who had once dwelt on the now split and tortured continent. It had been people like them that had built a nation. And if the nation was to return, it would be people like them that would rebuild it.

Jojo belched, savoring the mixture of gasses that flowed out of his belly. "Expensive," he asked.

Farkas laughed. "Of course."

Jojo looked at the slaves then looked beyond them. His eyes settled on a figure who was striding across the parade ground. It was one of his Radleps. And he was carrying some heavy burden slung over his shoulder.

Farkas followed the line of his guest's gaze. The 'lep pushed his way through the assembled slaves and carefully lay the dead 'lep at the feet of the masters of creation.

Farkas, his wife, and Jojo looked at the dead 'lep's hideous head wound. The 'lep who had found his fallen comrade spoke for all of them.

"Boss," he said, speaking to Jojo, ignoring Farkas, "we got troubles . . ."

Up in the hills, Bonner and the Lash of the Little People were preparing for war. Weapons were cleaned, checked and cleaned again. Sights were carefully aligned, ammo belts gone over with meticulous care to see that every round was properly packed. Once the Lash and their leader were within the compound there would be no time for a jammed gun, a misspent round. Every bullet would count. As it was, a lot of the little guys knew they wouldn't be coming back. But had Floyd or Bonner said that any one of them could back out then, no questions asked, no disgrace incurred, not one of the tiny fighters would have taken the deal. They were positively panting to get into the fight, to shed the blood of their enemies.

Bonner was ready. His shotgun was cleaned and oiled, his Steyr loaded, his knives strapped into place. He would have liked to go over the engine of his war wagon a little, but no one could do any tuning, for fear of attracting attention. The one thing he hadn't done was decide what to do with Bobby and Emily. He would like to have left them in the hills, but there was no guarantee that he could stop to rescue them as they all hauled ass out of the valley. No one, not even the most optimistic Lashman, could pretend that they were going to do anything more than make a lightning raid on the slave farm. They certainly could never capture it, leave alone hold it. They were going to go in, the little guys were going to steal as much as they could, Bonner was going to spring the slaves and then they were all going to get the hell out of there.

"Course, we'll set fire to the place," said Floyd.

"Course," said Bonner.

So what to do with the kids? He would like to have left them in the care of the Mean Brother. But Bonner couldn't do that again, not this time. Once the Mean was inside nothing was going to stop him looking for his brother. Nothing, except a direct order from Bonner, and Bonner didn't have the heart to give it. The kids, it seemed, were on their own. Bobby had demonstrated that he could take care of himself, but Emily? Bobby would have to look after his sister.

Bonner gave his Hi Standard to Bobby. "Use it," he said.

"I will," said Bobby. Bonner could tell by the look in his eye that the kid meant what he said.

Floyd ambled up and looked at the sky. "We go in as soon as it's dark, right?"

"Right," said Bonner.

"Given a thought to how we get through the gates?"

"Figured we'd ram 'em," said Bonner.

"We can't afford to get hung up outside, ya know. We gotta get in and start blastin'. If we get trapped outside them towers are gonna pour shot down on us like all fuckin' get out."

"Figure your war horse'll go through them gates?" asked Bunny who was standing nearby eavesdropping.

"She has to," said Bonner.

"You could use some sorta ram on the nose of that thing."

THE OUTRIDER

"Too late for that," said Bonner.

The Mean Brother thought otherwise, and without anyone noticing, he stole out the camp. He was gone for an hour or so, and when he returned, he carried on his back a huge old wrought iron gate, the kind that men like the ones that lived in houses like the one Farkas now occupied used to have on the driveways of their homes. The Mean Brother had trekked over to the neighboring plantation, now in ruins, found the gate, with its heavy, evil pointed spikes on top and carried back. If a ram was needed to reunite him with his brother, then he would find one.

Bonner smiled when he saw what the Mean Brother had found. "Good work," he said.

The Mean shrugged. A two-mile walk with a couple of hundred pounds of old iron on his back was not that big a deal to him.

He laid the gate across the hood of Bonner's car; the rusty spikes projected beyond the prow of the car a good three feet. Together, Bonner and the Mean lashed the ornate, deadly looking ironwork to the hood with rope. Bonner's car had never looked quite so unstoppable—or deadly.

"Still worried?" Bonner asked Bunny.

Bunny's rheumy blue eyes looked over the car, starting with fifty caliber in the stern and ending with the forest of spikes that thrust forward from the bow.

"Nope," he said.

The camp settled down to wait for the day light to fade and bring on the killing night.

166

*   *   *

The discovery of the dead 'lep had sent a shiver through the slave farm. Mrs. Farkas had sworn to herself. Things were going so good and then this had to happen. She could smell money—she knew that Jojo had tens of thousands of slates in his truck and she wanted them. Now, she thought, the fat fuck was spooked. He'd never deal now. All he wanted to do was get out of there, and he was demanding a huge escort—one so large that if there were any marauders up in the hills they would be able to walk in and take the slave farm if her husband acquiesced to Jojo's demands and sent most of the Devils out with Jojo's column.

"Man," shrieked Jojo, "do you know what that is?" He pointed at the dead lep. "Ferchrissakes, that was a Psycholep. A Psycholep! There is nothing meaner or tougher, do you read me on that? Nothing. Whoever is out there, man, is a fucking killer. I say again, there is no worse animal than a Psycholep!"

Except for the gent that parted his head, thought Mrs. Farkas, a little unkindly.

"Look," said Farkas soothingly. "You go take a nap . . ."

"A NAP!" screamed Jojo, as if unable to believe his ears.

"Yeah, you go take a snooze. I'll send some boys out to look around. If there's anybody out there, they'll take care of it."

"It ain't just anybody out there," said Jojo, fighting to keep the panic out of his voice. "It's Bonner and who knows what freaks he has with him."

"My boys can take care of anybody."

Jojo folded his arms over his tits and looked at Farkas as if he was crazy. "Sure," he said.

"Look—take a nap. Then we'll have a bite to eat, and then we'll put on a really great show for you."

"Spaghetti-Os?" asked Jojo hopefully.

"Yeah, yeah," said Farkas, "anything you want."

What a pair of morons, thought Mrs. Farkas.

Chapter Nineteen

Darkness came late on those summer nights, so Jojo
was able to sleep for several hours before being roused
by one of his personal 'lep bodyguards.

The 'lep moved into the room quietly and looked at
the sleeping Jojo for a few minutes. The disgust that
the scarred but steel-hard man felt for the gently
snoring fat man showed plainly on his battle-hardened
features. Jojo was not popular with the 'leps at the
best of times, and was even less so now that he hadn't
given the order immediately to revenge the death of
their fallen comrade. It was only the 'lep column's
personal oath to the Leatherman that allowed Jojo to
live at that very moment. Things would not always
be so simple as things were then. One day Leather
would get tired of Jojo and it would be the end of the
fat fuck, thought the 'lep. There was even talk that,

should there be a firefight on the way home Jojo just might, quite by accident, stop a stray slug. These things happen on the road. Leather would be the first to realize that.

"Time to get up, boss," said the 'lep.

Jojo snorted awake and sat up. "Huh?"

"Dinnertime," said the 'lep through cracked lips.

"Oh, good," said Jojo. He wiped his hand across his sweaty face. "Did Farkas send out patrols?"

"Yeah," said the 'lep.

"Any luck?"

"Nope."

"Fuck."

The 'lep turned to leave.

"Wait a minute . . ." The 'lep stopped and turned.

"Waddya think?" said Jojo, "ya think there's somebody out there?"

"Yeah," said the 'lep.

"Who? Bonner?"

"Yeah. We seen him, didn't we?"

"You don't think he'll be crazy enough to attack here, do you."

"Dunno," said the 'lep. "We all seen that man try just about anything."

"Well," said Jojo, heaving himself up off the bed, "if you see him, blast him."

The 'lep nodded. What the hell did the fat fuck think he was going to do if he saw him?

Dinner was another long, leisurely affair. Jojo chomped and grunted his way through seven courses, demanding second and third helpings of just about everything. Farkas made sure that there was plenty of his special home-brewed liquor around—the drink pleased Jojo almost as much as the food—so by the time they finished the meal, a few hours after they sat down, Jojo was in a pretty good frame of mind. He had almost forgotten the danger in the hills, his apprehension having been washed away in a tidal wave of food and drink. He was looking forward to whatever show it was that Farkas had planned, and was already looking beyond it. Maybe Farkas had a couple of good-looking chicks that he could take to bed that night to complete the circle of pleasures that had begun with his meal.

Farkas nodded to a slave who vanished only to reappear on the parade ground with a half dozen other slaves, each holding a flaming torch. These men walked slowly around the wide space of open ground, lighting larger torches that were stuck in the ground. By the time the twenty beacons were lit, the parade ground had been lit up as bright as day. The heavy pitch on the torch poles guttered, crackled, and spat. The elite of the slave farm, the head overseers, the Silk commanders, the 'leps, gathered on the verandah around the Farkas and Jojo, looking out onto the brightly illuminated ground as if they were patrons at one of the old pre-bomb theaters.

Outside the ring of light the rest of the slave farm gathered, huddled in the darkness, ready, with bright eyes, to watch the show.

"Looks good already,' said Jojo. He took a slug of malt liquor in the goblet at his elbow. Farkas had given a slave instructions that the glass was never to stand empty.

"You ain't seen nothing yet," said Farkas, rubbing his hands.

The evening's entertainment began with a boxing match. Six of the younger slaves were brought into the center of the pool of light and at the ringing of a bell, began a six-way slugging match. But it was more than a simple fistfight. Strapped across their knuckles were heavy pieces of lead that, when striking bone, shattered and crushed the limbs of their opponents. In that small, crowded ring, fists became fearsome weapons. As each blow landed, bones splintered and faces sagged. It was interesting to watch the shifting round of alliances between the young men; one or two joined forces to defeat the others, only to betray one another, to forge a new union with someone else and then turn on their former ally.

As the first punch was thrown, the crowd began screaming for blood, for pain. The excited voices of the onlookers drifted up from the circle of light, up into the night sky. The guards in the towers looked away from their posts craning their necks to get a better view of the action.

It seemed as if a muscled blond slave, not the biggest man in the ring but the fastest on his feet, would prevail. He chose his targets carefully, dancing in to land a bone-crunching blow on a chin, and simultaneously smacking his opponent a weighty blow on the knee. Two fighters doubled over in pain as the quick blond struck. But as he went in for the kill he was hit a powerful one-two from behind. Two lead-coated fists crashed into his body. One cracked the back of the skull, bringing out a syrupy flow of blood from a torn scalp, the other landed right at the base of his spine, fracturing the heavy medallion of bone that anchored his backbone.

The crowd screamed with delight as he fell. His finesse had not made as good a show as brute strength.

"Poor fuck," screamed Jojo, really getting into it, "he didn't follow the number one rule." No one asked him what it was so he supplied the answer himself. "Cover your ass!"

The brawny slave that had laid out the fast one now looked to be the winner until a lucky right from one of his smaller opponents smashed his jaw. The big guy fell in a shower of fine tissue from his lips and tongue. The two remaining slaves pounded him mercilessly as he went down. They didn't want him to get up again. He didn't.

The two boxers left circled each other warily. Each was losing blood from a half a dozen places where blows had only grazed their flesh. They staggered slightly from fatigue. The crowd screamed. They wanted more.

One figured they might as well get it over with. He lunged, fists windmilling. He sailed straight into a long, low, heavy blow to the ribs. It looked as if the bones broke around the iron-heavy fists. He fell, blood spurting from his mouth. The remaining boxer raised his hands above his head and danced a few steps to show that he was fresh as a daisy, ready for more.

Unfortunately, he failed to watch his vanquished victims. One of them, half dead from a broken jaw was jerked into a sort of consciousness by the roar of the crowd. He looked up, dazed, and saw that the fight was over. Without really thinking about it, he summoned what strength he had left and sent a lead-gloved fist into the winner's groin. The scream he let out soared above the laughter of the crowd. He toppled and curled around his broken private parts.

"No good for the stud sheds, huh, Farkas?" laughed Jojo.

"No," said Farkas. He was not pleased with that little development at all. It was one thing to pound a slave into a coma. It was another thing altogether to fuck up his regenerative organs. They were the most valuable thing about the livestock, the ability to make more. Oh well, thought Farkas, one less wouldn't break him.

The next act was taking its position center stage. These were five or six women, each naked to the waist and equipped with razor-sharp talons on the end on all ten fingers. Strapped to their feet were single-pointed blades.

"Catfight!" screamed the crowd in delight.

The women circled one another, snarling and

screeching, more like wild animals than people. Jojo feasted on their glistening oiled bodies. This *was* some show, he had to admit.

Without warning, one of the women lunged. The unfortunate object of her attack was caught off guard. Suddenly, the soft field of breast and stomach was a ribbon-slashed mass of blood. Gore-drenched talons ripped and tore. The dun-colored, flame-lit ground soaked up bright red blood, the yells of the crowd absorbed the tormented wails of the fighters. One of the women was whirling through the crowd of combatants like a maniac, slicing, slashing at anything that moved. One of her opponents took careful aim and kicked her hard, mid-stomach, the puncturing tool attached to her foot sliding deep into the crazy woman. As she fell she pulled her attacker down with her. As the two hit the drenched ground the others fell upon them, kicking them full of bloody holes.

One of the kickers broke off the attack long enough to lacerate the head and shoulders of the woman next to her. She fell, only to receive the punishment being meted out to the two that had fallen before her.

Two women were locked in a death struggle. Each had buried her claws in the back of the other and they wrestled in the dirt, their hideous blades rocking back and forth in the flesh of the other. It was sheer pigheadedness that kept the two bestial creatures locked together. Neither would release the other; both would die of their wounds.

A lone woman stood watching them wrestle in the

dirt. She had won. She was streaming with blood, her hair caked with the gore of others. Blood streamed down between her breasts. But she had won. All she had to do was deliver the two death blows. She drew back her right foot and knifed one woman in the back of the neck. The spike cut through the flesh and cartilage, the point splitting the skin on the other side of her neck. A great wash of warm blood spurted from her into the face of her opponent. The standing woman casually walked around behind the other, still enfolded in the death embrace of her enemy and split her skull with a swift kick to the back of the head. She extracted her embedded foot with some difficulty and then looked to Mr. and Mrs. Farkas.

"What do you think dear?" asked Farkas.

Mrs. Farkas looked at the blood-spattered creature. Her red breasts heaved, her strong bare legs ran with the blood of her enemies. Flesh had collected on the spikes on her feet. He blood dripping talons hung at her side.

"I dunno," said Mrs. Farkas. "she had it awful easy. Them two cunts going down like that . . . They handed her the victory."

Farkas shrugged at the slave woman. "Sorry, dear."

Mrs. Farkas reached up into her luxuriant hair, pulled out a handful of knives and with an unerring eye launched them in the direction of the catfight victor.

The woman fell screaming, cut down by a steel hailstorm.

Jojo was unmoved. "Thems the breaks," he said philosophically.

A hush came over the crowd. From behind the assembled gathering came a group of Silk Devils. It was time for the star attraction, the big event of the night. The Devils were forcing their way through the crowd, guns at the ready. The slave farm was used to shows involving dueling slaves—and they could be handled. This new attraction couldn't be taken care of by a few skag-men: this operation required care.

Jojo, Farkas, and Mrs. Farkas looked on eagerly as the captured Mean Brother was elbowed into the circle of light. The big man glowered around him, his upper lip curled in a ferocious sneer. He looked deep into Farkas' eyes, then at Mrs. Farkas, then over to the 'leps, and then, finally, at Jojo. The elite of the slave farm—except the 'leps of course—shifted uncomfortably.

Farkas broke the mood. "If looks could kill . . ." Jojo and Mrs. Farkas tittered nervously at the joke.

The Mean Brother looked calmly at them. He was confident that before the night was done he would kill. And with something a little more painful than simply a look.

Chapter Twenty

The Mean Brother cast a long shadow in the torchlight.
He towered over the surrounding bloodcrazed onlookers. They screamed and cried out and yelled,
anxious to see the Mean put through his paces. Not
one of them thought for a moment that they were in
any kind of danger. There were so many soldiers
around that the Mean Brother didn't stand a chance
of escape. All he was to them now was the star of
tonight's show. He would put out a good performance,
maybe a classic, and then, like all the others who
performed that night, he would die. But the final
curtain was many hours off yet. The night was young.

The Mean looked around him coolly. He looked
from howling face to howling face and firmly marked
this one and that one for death. When the fighting
started, the Mean had every intention of taking a few

dozen of his captors, his tormentors with him. They couldn't tell what he was thinking: if they could have, a lot of them would have foregone tonight's show and taken themselves away to a nice safe place, many miles from the Mean's dispassionate stare.

Farkas stood up and held up his hand for silence. Gradually the crowd settled down. The boss wanted to speak.

"Okay," he said, "settle down . . ." He waited expectantly for silence. "Okay," he said finally, "this is how it is. What we got here is one class A-type freak. Anybody ever seen a specimen like this before? Turn 'im around so the folks can get a look," he ordered. A couple of Devils approached and prodded the Mean Brother with rifle butts. The Mean, who had been given back his dignity by Bonner a long time before, refused to budge. The Devil dug at him with their shooters, slamming the Mean's rock-hard flesh. Still he refused to move. It was as if he was cemented to the spot.

"Okay," said Farkas, "I guess you can all see him . . ." He mentally added a horror or two to the stubborn giant's soon-to-be-painfilled end. "Anyway, we're gonna have a little fun with our big friend here, maybe a little rough but he looks like he can put up with some rough stuff, don't he?" It was a joke and everybody laughed as they knew they were supposed to.

Farkas shifted on his feet. "Now, I don't know that I personally would call this big freak a man, but

I can only see one set of feet, and he is standing on them, so I guess we gotta assume that he ain't no animal.''

The crowd laughed again. Farkas once again held up his hand for silence.

"However, it just so happens that we got ourselves a beast just as big as this one here and bein' that this one we got has four legs I guess we gotta believe it's not a human been. But what we don't know is who's tougher. You decide. And may the best *thing* win."

With that the ranks of Devils parted and a black bull, a raging, snorting beast with the fire of a life or captivity shining in its crazy eyes came thundering through the crowd.

The Mean Brother had just enough time to crouch and set his feet firmly in the dirt before the bull thundered down on him. The head was lowered, the horns out and aimed at the Mean. The man stepped out of the way of the rushing creature. As it passed, the Mean Brother smashed his big fist into the solid jawbone of the roaring beast.

The bull's hooves tore up a two-yard furrow in the hard ground. He stopped on the edge of the crowd and stood quivering with rage, staring at the Devils that swarmed around him with sharpened poles. The bull tossed his head and turned.

The bull had identified the Mean Brother as the enemy. He pawed the ground for a moment then charged again. The Mean Brother set directly in the path of the huge animal, then smacked it again as it pounded past. This time, though, he had struck the bull on the back of the neck, where the skull meets the spine. The bellowing animal staggered a few steps, then plunged into the crowd before him, tossing a helpless Devil on his horns. The man flew screaming into the air and then fell with a thud at the bull's hooves. The bull dipped down his great head and tore a ragged hole in the man's side. He screamed in terror as he watched his blood pumping out onto the gore-sodden, torn-up ground.

A crew of twenty Devils descended on the animal prodding it with their poles, trying to push it back towards the Mean Brother.

"Go get the big fucker," yelled one of the Devils. The bull appeared to do a little dance on the bleeding body of the fallen Devil. The man was crushed and broken in a dozen places. Sharp shards of bone sliced through his skin. His mouth was open, but no sound issued from his tortured lips. His pain was beyond expressing.

The smell of blood got mixed up in the hot fury of the animal brain. He turned, ready to claim the Mean Brother.

Both man and beast knew that this pass would be the last for one of them. There was the pure, white-hot desire to kill in each other's eyes. In a few seconds one of them would be dead. The bull pawed the ground and advanced, slowly at first, then gathering speed. The massive head went down, the evil points of the horns strained forward, ready to tear ghastly, bloody holes in the Mean Brother's big body.

Just when the bull was upon him, the Mean Brother reached out and grabbed the murderous horns in his superhuman grip. Then he launched his huge form off the ground, arching over the bull's head, pulling the creature to one side. As the Mean hit the ground, he kicked with all his might at the bull's forelegs, knocking those granite hard pilars out from under the big beast. The bull fell over, his hind legs kicking into the air.

The Mean was on top of him in a flash, pounding the bull's high ribcage. The bull tossed his head, trying to free his horns. But he couldn't break the grip of the Mean Brother. The Mean wrenched the big head to one side, forcing the slathering mouth onto the bloody ground. The bull tasted death.

Then the Mean flexed his muscles and threw himself into the air, dropping his huge weight, knee first, onto the jawbone of the bull. There was a sound like new timber cracking. The bull's eyes bulged. Froth shot from the animal's tortured mouth. A great plug of snot poured from the flared nostrils. Then the head lolled back.

There was silence from the crowd which a second before had been screaming.

"He broke its fuckin' neck," whispered someone. The crowd stared, as if not quite able to believe what it had witnessed.

The Mean Brother jumped off the warm carcass and stood looking defiantly at Farkas. Then the big man walked to the edge of the circle of onlookers and drew a knife from the sheath that was strapped to a Devil's thigh. With that he carved the tongue from the bull's mouth, holding the bloody foot-long piece of flesh up for all to see. Then he tossed in into Farkas' lap. It landed with a warm, wet slap on the big man's lap.

Farkas jumped to his feet. "You motherfucker!" A stain of blood six inches across soaked his pants at crotch level.

"Kill the fucker!"

A dozen Devils jumped into the ring, each carrying a club or a length of chain. They marched toward the Mean Brother.

One wanted to be a hero. He swung his chain in a furious arc, hoping to succeed with one blow where a seven-hundred-pound bull had failed. The Mean reached out and grabbed the chain and reeled in the Devil, pulling the man up to his face, so the soon-to-be-dead tough guy could get a good look at the Mean Brother's face and know as he expired that he never, never, stood a chance.

The sledgehammer fist that capped the Mean Brother's right arm smashed into the Devil's throat, making a confused, bruised, and useless hash of that bundle of windpipe and veins. If the Devil lived, he would never speak again. But he wouldn't live. The sharp cords of his larynx had penetrated the carotid artery. He would lose enough blood in the next few minutes to pass out. A minute after that, he would die.

The others faltered for a second.

"I said kill the fuck," screamed Farkas. "I'm gonna personally shoot any man that leaves that ring alive!!"

Jojo hardly heard Farkas' screams. This was one hell of a night. Jojo considered himself something of a sports connoisseur. He didn't react when the 'lep behind his chair, nudged his shoulder trying to get his attention.

"Boss," he rasped.

"Don't bother me," snapped Jojo.

The 'leps had heard it, but no one else had. Almost as one man, they unslung their weapons and put a fresh round in the chamber.

The Mean Brother had felled another of his attackers with a cruel blow to the balls. The man's testes had been crushed to paste and his wailing split the night.

The Devils figured that there was only one way to bring down the Mean and that was to rush him, all at once. Clubs and chains flailing they came at him. The Mean took an arm-numbing blow to the forearm, but he brushed it off. He could not allow pain to get in his way. He was fighting not just for survival, but for something much more important than that. He was fighting for vengeance and there was nothing more crucial in his life than that simple commodity.

The Mean punched out at a Devil, laying him out with a single blow. As the man fell, The Mean Brother snatched the man's weapon from him, a chain. Thus armed, and with his huge arms working like pistons, the Mean struck down two more of his enemies. With each crack of steel against flesh the Mean seemed to become stronger. It was as if he robbed his enemies of their life and took it to himself, using their strength to kill more.

The chain was slick with blood and flesh and the Mean stood in the midst of a heap of writhing bodies, each cringing and crying out from the force and shock of hideous wounds.

The Mean had taken some punishment, too. Blows had rained down on his head and shoulders, stripping large patches of hairy skin from his huge form. He streamed not just with the blood of his enemies but his own, too. In this he felt ashamed. He had never been challenged so. That he was winning was not enough. He had to win with ease. It was a Mean Brother credo that no enemy was worthy, no enemy capable of inflicting pain.

That thought pulsed through his brain as a white-hot fury seized him. To those watching, it seemed as if the already massive Mean Brother grew in size. The desire to kill had so completely suffused him that it gave him new strength.

His attackers, more fearful of the Mean Brother than Farkas' bullets saw the change come over the man-giant and they drew back.

The crowd, Farkas, Jojo, were suddenly scared. The Mean looked around him, as if choosing where next he would strike.

"Wha . . . what's he gonna do?' stammered Jojo.

"Kill the fuck!" bellowed Farkas. "Shoot him down!"

Only the 'lep on the balcony reacted to the suggestion fast enough to bring their weapons to bear. The Mean Brother reached down scooped up a couple of the broken bodies at his feet and flung them into the knot of 'leps. The Radleps staggered back and fired wildly, just as the Mean Brother dove into the mixed crowd of Devils, overseers, and slaves who had been watching the show.

The chatter of automatic fire from the maddened leps cut through the crowd. Bullets splattered into a dozen bodies adding to the already horrifying body count of the evening.

The Mean Brother swam into the darkness.

"Find him!" screamed Farkas, "kill him. Kill him!"

The parade ground became a confused crush of men and women screaming, dashing for cover, crying out for help, nursing wounds. The men in the towers peered at the crazy crowd wondering who to shoot at.

"Boss," hissed a 'lep in Jojo's ear, "boss, we're gonna be attacked. Engines, we heard engines."

"Engines? What engines?" demanded Jojo.

It was at that moment that Bonner's car crashed through the front gate of the slave farm. The long bloody night would go on for a lot longer, and get a lot bloodier before it had run its course.

Chapter Twenty-one

As they made their way down the mountain, the roar of the crowd in the camp, plainly audible over the noise of the engines, and the bright pool of light in the middle of the slave farm told Bonner that there was something big happening in Farkas' little horror haven. They were almost on top of the slave farm before anyone in the guard towers heard them, and even then the Devils did not open fire. They had swung their few heavy weapons around to face within the camp and had trouble muscling them back to face forward in time to catch the onrushing riders. By the time they were ready to open up, the savage vengeance seekers were already inside the compound.

"HOLD ON!" shouted Bonner to the Mean Brother and the two kids that rode with him. The points of the old iron gate smashed into the wire that blocked the entrance to the slave farm. A second later the weight of Bonner's war wagon crashed into the tough wire and wood frame and, with a hard stamp on the accelerator, the behemoth machine smashed a gaping hole in the gate. A tangled skein of wire broke over the car and the engine screamed its annoyance at being so terribly mistreated.

Bonner urged the car on a few yards, feeling, with his instinctive sense for machinery, that while he had banged his iron maiden around once again it had served him in grand style. The engine fired as if he was shooting down the open road, the chassis remained firm and untwisted, despite the jarring blow it had received.

Bonner had time to glance over his shoulder to see a hoard of Lashmen swarming like maddened bees through the gap he had gouged open.

Then he hit his spotlight. The night opened up.

Before him all was confusion. The crowd bucked and parted like a spooked herd of wild horses on the stampede. Bonner heard the sporadic chatter of automatic fire. A thought flashed through his mind: 'Leps, they always keep their head, because they are not afraid to die.

It seemed like the Lashmen were everywhere. The fearless little fighters scythed into the maddened crowd. It was impossible to tell how many Devils they brought down on that bloody first strike.

To an outside observer it might seem that the Lashmen were an undisciplined force—and, to be honest, sometimes they were. But this time they moved with precision. Once through the gates, they all knew the job that each had to perform.

The first few Lashmen, Floyd and Rufus in the fore, charged the bucking, crazed mass of people. The idea was to cause maximum confusion: maximum confusion equaled maximum damage. They swept through the crowd, hands off their handlebars, a firing weapon in each hand. That way, no one in the defending camp could tell exactly how many men had attacked them. The way the first Lashmen were going about it, cutting down a Devil with virtually every shot, it seemed like the farm had been attacked by a hundred well-armed, well-trained men.

The next batch of midgets through the gates, stopped dead in their tracks, jumped off their powerful little machines, and started pumping fire at the surprised guards in the gate towers. Theirs was a threat that had to be neutralized immediately. Heavy automatic weapons, recoilless rifles, and the like were rare in the new world. The damage they could inflict could be substantial. Once the battlelines were firmly drawn Bonner and Floyd wanted to make sure that if any firepower was pouring out of those towers, it had to be aimed at Devils. The guns had to be knocked out, or, even better, captured.

The last bunch through the gate was, to the Lashmen's way of looking at things, probably the most important. They were to ignore the fighting altogether and make straight for the house. They had to find what portable booty Fakas had lying around, steal it, and blast their way out. The Lashmen trusted each other. They had to. The men detailed to stealing anything Farkas had to offer would not wait for the battle to end, they had to grab and run. They would all meet up later and divide the spoils.

Bonner knew where he was headed. And the Lashmen knew it was his own special role to play. He was going to make straight for the slave sheds and start letting them out. The slaves would break for freedom, even if it meant walking into the firestorm that the Lash and Bonner had created outside. Hot steel was better than a lifetime of torment at Farkas'.

The 'leps too knew they had a job to do. They nestled on the parapet of the balcony and started returning the fire of the Lashmen. They pumped bullets into the killing ground in front of them, but found it hard to hit the tiny targets that kept moving. Bullets hit Devils, they hit slaves, but they had a hard time finding the Lashmen.

A midget popped up from behind a pile of Devil corpses and blew a 'lep head clean off. Like one man, six Radleps aimed for the spot where the little guy had been and let fly.

But he wasn't there.

Roaring in frustration, a 'lep jumped up onto the wide banister that fronted the balcony and blasted away a fast series of rips from his M-16. The slugs chewed up an acre of recently dead flesh, but hit no Lashmen. But a dozen hidden rifles had taken careful bead on the 'lep. His body seemed to explode as round after round tore into his exposed flesh.

The 'leps, seeing yet another of their number fall, cried out in shame and anguish. The battle at Farkas' slave farm was shaping up as a major 'lep defeat. If the remaining 'leps didn't kill each and every member of the attacking force . . . well, there was no telling what Leatherman would do.

The group of Lashmen detailed to knocking out the towers had the situation well in hand. The chatter of automatic weapons fire continually splintered the wood around the tower tops, causing the Devils within to keep their heads down or risk losing them.

Suddenly a tiny figure broke from the group that was clustered around the gate posts making life miserable for the guards in the towers. With a knife clenched in his teeth and a huge side arm in one tiny hand, the midget began to climb, one handed, up the spindly legs of the tower. Here, at last, was a target for the assembled 'leps.

A sickening wave of lead-woven fire washed over the little figure who clambered up the side of the tower. Wood splintered and flew and the midget was hit in every quarter of his body. He hung for a moment, his bloody fingers scrabbling on the smashed wood for a handhold. But the weight of his injuries sapped his strength and he fell to the ground, dead.

But the tower had to be taken—every Lashmen

knew it. As soon as the first attacker had fallen to the ground another had jumped up to take his place. His fellows on the ground provided covering fire. Bonner saw the drama unfold and saw a 'lep stand and carefully line up the climbing Lashman in the sights of his shooter. Bonner's beautiful shotgun sprung into his hands and he launched a twin barrelled load of double O buck magnum, cutting the evil sonofabitch in half. Then the Outrider went about his business.

The midget on the tower had reached the top. He leaped over the low guard rail and ended the lives of the four Devils crouched there. The little man pushed two of the bodies together and then, using the corpses as a firing step put the big recoilless rifle that was mounted there to good use. The leps suddenly felt a large caliber hot rain falling on them.

The big shells tore gouts out of the masonry that provided protection and the bodies it protected. The 'leps did something the 'leps aren't supposed to do. They took cover, flat on their stomachs.

With his primary target out of sight, the midget in the tower turned the gun on the twin of the tower he was in. A few yards away, across the narrow entrance way stood the other tower, its crew still alive, but hiding. The huge gun barked and ripped a few strips off the wooden wall that provided the guards with their only cover. The next clip cut them to pieces.

A squad of Devils had run into the house and had taken up positions in the upper windows. From here they had a commanding view of the parade ground. They had managed to pin down the Lashmen who were supposed to penetrate the house and begin looting. That squad, ten in all, commanded by Bunny, were taking serious casualties. They had lost five and another two or three were wounded.

"We ain't gonna make it," screamed one of the Lashmen. Bunny's experienced eyes swept the parade-ground. Not a lick of cover. His comrade just might be right. Bullets ripped up the ground around him. "Shit," he said quietly.

The formerly captive Mean Brother had darted around behind the house, smashed a window, and climbed into what was obviously a kitchen. A few house slaves cowered there trying to force themselves behind a huge old coal stove. They stared at the Mean, still dripping with blood, sure that their tortured lives were about to end. Suddenly, their worthless lives seemed very valuable.

But the Mean Brother had no interest in them. He swept by them, pausing only to pick up a large kitchen knife, which he stuck in the belt of his pants, and a heavy frying pan. In his other hand he held the chain he had taken from one of his attackers. He stole into the house.

He heard the firing from upstairs and slowly began climbing the wide staircase.

The rest was easy. There was a series of bedrooms leading off a wide corridor. In each there were a couple of Devils, all staring intently out the window, blasting away at the parade ground. The first two did not hear the Mean Brother enter. One took a superhuman blow from the chain around the neck. The other got cracked with the frying pan. He died with the sound of the dull "bong" of cast iron whacking his skull.

The Mean went into the next room. Three Devils at the window. One throat cut with the kitchen knife, two others sent on their way to hell with the frying pan. The next room yielded two more Devils. As the Mean entered, something made one of the shooters turn. He collected the full weight of the pan in the face. The heavy smack from the pan caved in his nose and split the skin over both eyes. His companion had tried to bring his weapon to bear, but the long barrel had gotten caught up in the fussy drapes that Mrs. Farkas had hung all over the place.

The knife was buried handle deep into his chest. He stared unseeing at the black handle, the look on his face suggesting that he couldn't quite believe that all this was happening to him.

The firing from the windows gradually died down and Bunny didn't wait to see who or what had been his saviour.

"Let's move it, Lashmen!" he yelled and jumped forward, leading the way towards the open door of the house.

Mrs. Farkas was not a fool and she wasn't afraid of a fight either. She pulled a dainty Beretta pistol from an even smaller holster on her thin ankle and darted behind the upturned dinner table and began firing like a pro. She hit one of Floyd's attack squad, chuckling to herself as his little cycle careened out of control and smashed into one of the huts. The driver, a quiet little Lashman called Winston, died from a broken neck, although the slug that Mrs. Farkas put into him would have killed him eventually.

As the battle progressed, though, it became clear to the mistress of the slave farm that, even if she and her husband came out of this encounter alive, life was not going to be the same. Someone had fought his way to the slave sheds and their captives, their livestock, were free, running for their lives.

She also smelled smoke. Some of the outbuildings were burning. It was only a matter of time before the house caught. There was a brisk wind blowing. Undoubtedly, probably inevitably, the wind would carry sparks into the fields. By night's end, she was willing to bet, Farkas' little empire would be a raging inferno.

Mrs. Farkas was a tough broad and she was dry-eyed about the sudden death of her and her husband's business. Unemotional perhaps, but far from uncon-cerned. Right then, with the battle swirling and rag-ing around her, she swore vengeance on the men—the man—who had brought her so low. But that was for later—right now she had to see about getting out of there in one piece. Not an easy task.

Bonner had made straight for the slave sheds. He burst through the first door he came to and stopped.

The huge room was full of bunk beds with scores of pregnant women sprawled on them.

One of them saw this driven man, his face stained with the smoke and dirt of battle and screamed:

"Don't shoot! Please! My baby!"

"Don't worry." said Bonner. "Look, you can all escape, you can all get out of here . . ."

The swollen women stared at him, uncomprehending. "You're all free . . ."

"Free?" inquired one.

Bonner didn't have time for this. "Head out the back. Don't go towards the house."

A few figures stirred listlessly. Bonner headed for the door. Then something stopped him.

"I said *you're free*, you can go now."

It was the woman whom Farkas had singled out as his best breeder who answered him. "Mister," she croaked, "we can't go nowhere."

"What do you mean?"

"It don't matter. It just don't matter. Now you get out of here. Go. You done your best. You're just too late. You tried and we appreciate it."

Dozens of sad eyes regarded him. The old woman was right. Where could they go from here, these weary, exhausted, pregnant woman. He realized in a flash: he hadn't set them free, he had condemned them to death. Slavery had become their lives, they could never adapt to freedom. The eyes of those women would haunt him for the rest of his life. He crashed through the door hoping that he wasn't too late to save someone in that hell hole.

In the next room he found a small measure of salvation. There, flat on the floor to avoid the bullets that whistled through the flimsy planking of their hut, were the men and women of Almost Normal.

As soon as he burst through the door, every person in the room thought the same thing: This is the end, Farkas has sent someone to kill them all. It was Charlie who looked up, curious to see the men who would kill him.

Instead, his heart leaped as he recognized his friend Bonner as the man with the smoking cut-down shotgun in one hand and a murderous little chattergun in the other. In the instant he laid eyes on the Outrider, Charlie, a simple soul, realized that the man who had come to save them was action, discipline, controlled violence personified. Charlie was itching to get at the men who enslaved him and his wife and destroyed his town, his world, but he knew he would never be able to inflict the damage that The Outrider could.

"Bonner!"

"Charlie," barked Bonner. "You're taking your people out. Get out the door and head for the gate."

"Guns," said a man, "give us guns."

"You can pick up what you can find outside. But don't hang around. Don't look for guns. Look for a vehicle. And put as much distance as you can between you and this place as you can. We can't hold them forever."

"We can't leave you to fight our battle."

"It's not yours. It's mine. I started it." Bonner called over his shoulder. "Now let's go."

Bonner kicked open the door and took in the scene in front of him. The battle had stabilized. The Lashmen were still engaging pockets of Devils and—bad news—the 'leps had worked themselves out of their jam and were fighting with their trademark ferocity.

Bonner dived into the dirt and crawled a few yards away from the door. All he could do was set up some diversionary fire and allow the newly freed slaves to make a break for the vehicle park that stood off to one side of the compound. There were a couple of the convoy trucks parked there. He prayed silently that one of the Almost Normals knew the rudiments of driving.

"Let's move it!" Bonner yelled.

Running almost bent double the first of the men came out. Bonner sighted his Steyr AUG on a cluster of Devils who crouched at the base of the house and let fly. Four or five gun barrels turned in his direction and opened up. Bonner answered with hot fire, slicing into the group. He saw a couple of Devils fall in a tangle of arms and legs. Just behind behind him, Bonner hear the curious "phut" of bullet striking flesh. A man crumpled to the ground. It was one of the men from Almost Normal, one of the ones who would lose the gamble for freedom that night.

Bonner stood and, keeping himself between the escapees and the battle front, he escorted them across the paradeground. The needle nose of the Steyr seemed to point in every direction at once. Up at the roof line, into the trees that made up a portion of Farkas' garden, down to the ground where the Devils lay huddled behind anything that would give them cover. The Steyr spat bullets, carrying a swift, painful message of vengeance to every quarter of their battlefield. Bonner had become swept up in the conflict, his brain having given way completely to instinct. He had become the vengeance machine that ordinary men feared. He was now the unerring death dealer—to challenge him was to come to a sudden end. To run was to realize that there was no place to run to. His weapon had become an extension of himself, his mind grabbed hold of the minds of other men, anticipating their moves, sensing their fear, destroying them without effort. He had become a man of seamless action, forged in violence, tempered in revenge. Unstoppable.

The Almost Normals got to the trucks. The women huddled in the lee of an old pickup, clutching their children tight while the men raced through the lines of the vehicles searching for a machine that would start. Stray bullets whistled around them. A few were cut down.

Bonner was crouched next to an old rain barrel, singlehandedly engaging a group of Devils who had taken up positions on the roof of one of the slave sheds. He would dart out from his position for a second, whip a couple of Devils off the roof with a spray of automatic fire, then step back into the cover of his rusting barrel. Charlie appeared at his side.

"What are you doing here?" Bonner demanded.

"You didn't think I'd leave, did you."

"What the hell good do you think you're going to do. You've never been in a firefight."

"I can shoot. And I'm mad." As if to illustrate his words he blasted a Devil who had appeared at a window above them. The man had looked out as if to check on the weather. The bullet, followed by a hundred sharp shards of glass, lacerated his face.

"I gotta tell you," said Bonner, between bursts from the Steyr, "Bobby and Emily . . ."

"They're dead," said Charlie, as if long since resigned to the fact.

"No," said Bonner, "they're here. . . ."

As soon as Bonner had ground his car to a halt—it seemed as if it had been hours before, but was in fact about thirty minutes past—the Mean Brother had jumped out carrying his trademark axe. He was intent on finding his brother and wreaking his own brand of havoc on the men who had captured him. Bobby and Emily had been left behind. The two kids had climbed out of the machine and found cover by a pile of neatly cut cordwood. From there they had watched and fought. Bobby handled the Hi Standard well. His sister had been armed with a small Charter Pathfinder that didn't jump out of her small hands every time it went off. Together they brought down their fair share of bandits. They were both scared. Emily's hands trembled as she reloaded the small gun, but reload it she did and kept on blasting. They were well hidden and they laid down fire well—too well. They were looking directly onto a squad of Devils. One by one they dropped from the kids accurate fire. The leader of the squad, a big killer called Denny, couldn't figure out where the shots were coming from. The kids were making every shot count. With their light-caliber handguns they couldn't keep up a steady rate of fire. All they could do was take careful aim and fire. The constant chatter of larger weapons masked their deadly shooting.

Denny looked around, as much as he dared, and couldn't find the source of the marksmen. But he thought the woodpile looked awfully suspicious. The next time one of his guys dropped, Denny whipped around with his semiauto and peppered the neatly stacked wood. The firing stopped.

"That's where the fuckers are," he thought and got off on a belly crawl to kill whoever lurked behind there. A yard or two from the pile, he jumped to his feet and sprinted the last few feet, jumping up onto the stack, ready to kill. He looked down the barrel of his gun and saw two kids.

Somewhere at the back of his mean brain, a tiny spark of decency burned. It kept his finger off the trigger long enough for him to say:

"Kids?"

And long enough for Bobby to raise the Hi Standard and blow his face off.

Then they were out of bullets. "We gotta get more," said Bobby.

"Where?" said Emily. Tears clogged her throat.

Bobby peered over the woodpile. The battle ground was littered with the weapons of the fallen. "Out there."

"Okay," said his sister, "let's go."

Farkas had grabbed a weapon from a nearby Devil when they were attacked but he was too upset to use it. He had retreated to the big drawing room just behind the verandah, kicked over a couch, and had taken up a position behind it. Big hot tears streamed down his face.

"They're ruining everything!" he cried.

Jojo had crawled over the broken glass and torn up carpeting to where the slave owner hunched down.

"I'm telling you, Farkas," he said, "there is going to be trouble about this."

"Shut up, you fat asshole," said Farkas. He went on crying.

Bonner and Charlie burst into the room, looking for the kids.

"Hey," said Jojo, who had been cowering with Farkas for what seemed like days, "that's Bonner."

"Bonner?" said Farkas, like a man awakened from a dream. "Bonner? I hate him."

He raised his gun. "BONNER!" he screamed.

Bonner whirled, the Steyr telegraphing its deadly message. A neat row of bullets tore across Farkas' chest. He staggered back a foot or two, clawed at a curtain, and pulled it down on top of him. Bonner jumped onto the upturned sofa and found Jojo crouching there.

"Bonner man," whispered Jojo, "I mean, what can I say? I got money. I can make you rich . . ."

Very calmly, Bonner slipped the shotgun from the holster on his back. He lowered it until the two smooth, glinting barrels were level with Jojo's blubbering mouth.

"Anything, man, I can give you anything."

"Can you give me Leather?" asked Bonner quietly.

"Shit yeah!" said Jojo. He couldn't believe The Man, The Outrider would deal. "Yeah. I can give you Leather."

Bonner's strong right forearm absorbed all the kick of the heavy bore shotgun. The two shell splattered Jojo's head all over the wall. Bonner knew that Jojo couldn't give him Leather, he just wanted to see how far the fat rat would go to save his skin.

Charlie and Bonner sprinted up the steps and found Bunny and his men at the top of them. "It's un-fuckin'-believable, man, just unbelievable," babbled Bunny.

"What is?" demanded Bonner.

"Look."

Bonner and Charlie looked into the open door of a bedroom that stood off to their left. It was stacked, floor to ceiling with gold objects of every kind. Everything from finely worked pieces of pre-bomb jewelry to crudely pressed gold slates. It lay spread around, ankle-deep on the floor. It was Farkas' treasure, tons of precious metals taken from every slave he had ever captured, looted from riders long dead, stolen from the ruins of the old cities. It was a treasure that no one, not even Leather or Berger, could equal.

"Money," thought Bonner, "big deal."

Bunny's squad was loading as much loot as they could into sacks, pillowcases, bundles of sheets as they could. The Lashmen were going to set rich out of this raid.

"Look," said Bunny, "we gotta split. See ya in Chi-town."

"Been a pleasure, Bunny."

"All ours." The little men made for the stairs.

"Hey," called Bonner, "seen the kids?"

"Nope," said Bunny. "They're around here someplace."

"Great," said Charlie.

Emily grabbed a gun from the bloody ground and tried to sprint back to safety. A Devil saw her and brought her down with a flying tackle.

"You're my ticket outta here, honeypie," he hissed in her ear.

Emily shrieked and squirmed in the tight grasp of the Devil. She twisted, scratched and bit and when her teeth sunk into the fleshy part of the Devil's dirty hand, he yelped and dropped her. Emily raised her gun and fired. Unfortunately, she had picked up an ornery old bull of a handgun, twenty pounds too heavy, it seemed, for her spaghetti-thin wrists. She had to put her entire weight behind the stiff hard trigger. The pistol had a kick on it like a punch from a Mean Brother. It flew out of her hand as it went off, the big slug just barely grazing the Devil's shoulder. But it hurt. He lost his temper.

"BITCH!" he screamed and raised his own weapon. He took careful aim and fired. Emily screwed up her eyes waiting for the fatal slug. The gun failed to go off.

Caught by his own fury, the Devil raised his metal-shod boot. If he wasn't going to shoot her, he was going to stomp the little bitch.

Rufus had just finished cutting the throat of a hapless overseer who had just squealed and squirmed like a sliced pig. As he stood over his squirming, bleeding, expiring victim, he noticed the Devil preparing to kick Emily to death.

"Hey, motherfucker," he shouted, his voice hot with anger and indignation, "pick on someone your own fuckin' size!" Without pausing to consider that the Devil was at least two feet taller and two hundred pounds heavier, Rufus launched himself at Emily's attacker.

He put every pound of his weight behind his tackle and brought the Devil down. His knife was out and he was trying with all his might to drive the ugly blade deep into the Devil's chest.

"Take off, pussy, take off," he screamed over his shoulder at Emily.

Bruised and dazed, Emily struggled to her feet. She heard Rufus' order, but ignored it.

Rufus fought like a man possessed; he spat and kicked, but the weight of the Devil's strength was simply greater. He was facing the point of his own knife. The Devil slashed at Rufus' arm and the muscle and sinew of his biceps cracked and split under the blade. Emily retrieved her gun and thrust it between the locked bodies of the Devil and the midget. She jammed it between the Devil's lips and, two-handed, pulled the trigger.

Her adolescent voice screamed: "EAT THIS!" The Devil's head showered her and Rufus in a torrent of blood, brain, and bone.

Rufus staggered back, wiping gook from his face. "Tough chick," he said admiringly.

From the second story of the house, Charlie saw his daughter saved. He tore down the stairs and ran across the porch.

"Emily!" he called.

Emily swung around with her gun ready, a wild look in her once innocent eyes. She stared at her father for a moment, as if not able to recognize him. Then, the terror-filled days and nights caught up with her. For a second, as she ran into his arms, she was a little girl again. Bobby came running from the woodpile and the three of them hugged, rocking back and forth, while the battle raged around them.

Bonner watched from the window. His mouth set in grim line. He had done what he had set out to do. Palls of smoke were washing across the farm, some of the outbuildings were burning brightly, the house and the fields were beginning to catch.

Time to go.

Chapter Twenty-two

There was a brief meeting of the combatants a few miles from the slave farm. By the time Bonner and the reunited Mean Brothers arrived, the remains of the Lashmen had gotten there, so had the truck carrying the newly liberated Almost Normals.

They looked surprised, happy, shocked—unable to believe that they had escaped, that Bonner had come for them.

Charlie climbed down from the truck and took Bonner's hand. He shook it firmly.

"We'll never be able to thank you," he said, "never."

"Forget it," said Bonner.

"And finding my kids'n all . . ." Charlie's voice cracked with emotion, tears started into his eyes.

"They're good kids," said Bonner, "you should be proud."

Charlie turned from him. "Bobby! Emily! Come say good-bye."

The two children came over shyly, as if meeting Bonner for the first time. They paused a moment, then embraced him warmly.

"Take care," whispered Bonner. He wondered if they would ever be the same. Probably not.

"Okay, break it up," said Floyd. "If these folks are headed out to the westlands they better get moving. The Hotstates are gonna be jumping. And that's the truth . . ."

"Yeah," said Bonner, "you better get going."

Rufus grabbed Emily just before the truck moved out. His wrinkled, ugly face was folded into a big grin. "You saved my ass back there, sweetheart."

"You bet your ass I did," said Emily.

Rufus threw back his head and laughed. "Look me up when you're a little older, kid. We'll party . . ."

The truck went one way, Bonner and the Lashmen the other. They bombed down the highway, the Lashmen leading. Allowing for the squad that had already taken off for Chi-town with Farkas' loot, Bonner figured the Lash had been hurt bad. Only seven men rode ahead of him. Bonner felt bad about that. But every Lashman knew the risks.

Mrs. Farkas pushed the big truck over the hills. As she changed gear she shifted alternately from tears to extraordinary swearing. Farkas was dead, the farm was in ruins, they had lost virtually everything they owned.

But survival was second nature to Mrs. Farkas. She had taken a truck, but she didn't take just any old truck. She had taken Jojo's truck. And in the back, among all the pillows and food, she had found the money that Jojo had planned to spend on slaves. It wasn't close to the amount she lost, but it was a start. Mrs. Farkas knew exactly what she was going to do with it: she was going to build herself a gang and find the man that had ruined her life. That was a promise. . . .

Bonner's big engine had pulled him ahead of the Lashmen: soon he was alone on the road. As he cut along the open highway, bound for home, he saw a tiny figure ahead of him on the highway.

It was Wiggy, the little rider that Bonner had traded with, meat for ammunition. The man was staggering along under the weight of a fly-blown side of beef. It stunk. He heard the powerful engine behind him and paled.

"Omigod!" he said and scuttled behind a junked, rusty old family sedan. He chanced a look down the road and saw Bonner.

"Oh no," he whispered, "him . . ."

Bonner cruised to a halt next to the shell of the car. Wiggy raised his head warily. "Hi," he said.

Bonner smiled. "Hi."

"What can I do for you?" asked Wiggy.

"Nothing," said Bonner.

"Nothing?"

"Just thought you might like a ride."

"Hell, yeah," said Wiggy.

"Hop on," said Bonner. "Ah, leave the meat . . ."

They bombed down the road, Wiggy reclining in the back, already planning his story for Pershing's Pistoleros. "Yeah, I hooked up with Bonner down in the Hotstates and me'n Bonner see . . ."

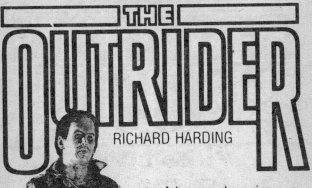